BURIED TREASURE

DEE'S MYSTERY SOLVERS

LEONARD D. HILLEY II

Illustrated by

SELFPUBBOOKCOVERS/FANTASYART

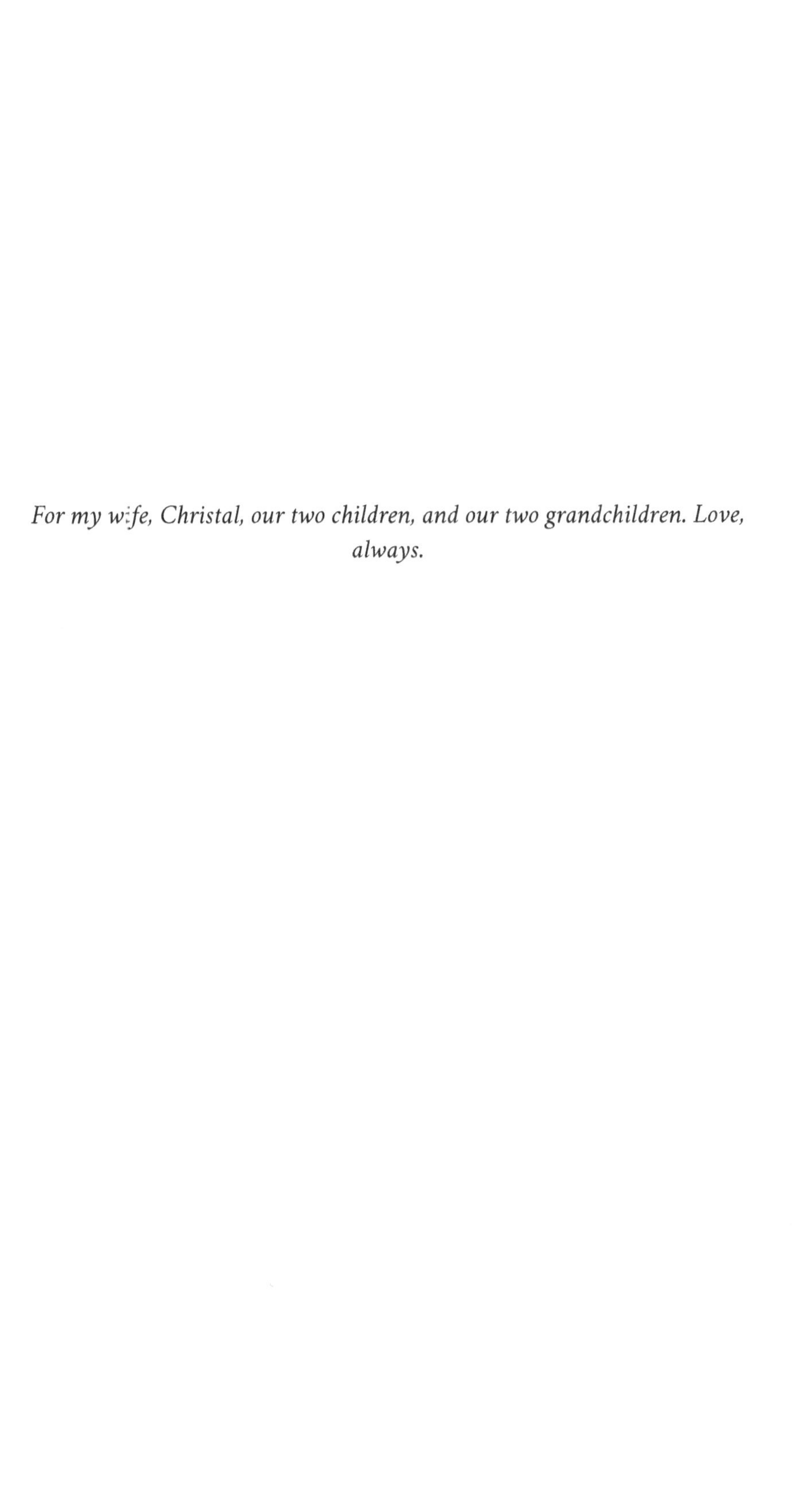

For my wife, Christal, our two children, and our two grandchildren. Love, always.

CHAPTER 1

"Order! Order!" Dee hammered the podium with her father's rubber mallet. "Let's call this meeting to order!"

"None of us are even talking, Dee," Marty said, grinning and shaking his head. Sitting on a metal barstool, he glanced at the other two members of The Mystery Solvers Club.

Lynn and Adam laughed. Adam plopped on the old beanbag chair, sending a cloud of dust lofting around him. He coughed and fanned the dust away with his hand. Lynn slid on a tool bench, trying to suppress her laughter.

Dee frowned, shook her head, and her bobbed hair swayed side to side.

"She gets a little carried away, doesn't she?" Adam asked, wiping dust from his face.

"A *little*?" Marty cocked a brow.

"So my excitement's gotten the best of me. Sue me," Dee said with a shrewd grin.

"Why are you so excited?" Lynn said. She took a brush from her purse and ran it through her glossy black hair. Her favorite scarlet ribbon she used to tie her ponytail lay folded across her knee.

"No one *looked* at this morning's paper?" Dee asked.

"Duh, no," Adam said, crossing his arm. "School's still out so I'm reserving my reading time for when classes start back and teachers *force* us to read."

Lynn chuckled. "Well, that explains the '*duh*.' No need to *overwork* your brain."

Adam gave her a harsh side-glance.

Marty glanced at the rolled newspaper in Dee's hand. "So what's the news, Sis?"

Dee grinned and unfolded the paper on the podium. "It took us a lot of time to work on that petition for Ms. Cooper at the library."

"Did … it … ever," Adam exasperated a sigh and rolled his eyes. "Two weeks of door-to-door knocking and pleading, and we were *still* thirty-six signatures short."

"But our effort was worth it," Dee replied.

"How?" Adam sat up and turned his ball cap backwards. He might have looked tougher if he wasn't sunk in the beanbag chair. "We didn't reach our quota."

"With the help of a church lady who wanted to post a flyer at the library for their Cake Walk, Ms. Cooper got the church members to sign the petition, putting us about a dozen signatures *over* the 500 we needed."

"So what's next?" Marty asked.

"The newspaper interviewed Ms. Cooper and she says that at next week's meeting, she'll present the petition before the council," Dee said. "Apparently the reporter who did the interview was on our side, so she's painted the importance of having those graves exhumed and placed into Ravenswood Cemetery, and as she puts it, 'Imagine if these were your ancestors. Wouldn't you want to be able to pay your respects to them? Moving their graves is the decent thing to do.'"

"Great news!" Marty said.

Lynn nodded, taking black lipstick from her purse.

Dee grinned. "You bet it is. We're even mentioned in the article."

"We are?" Adam said, rising slightly. "We're celebrities in—"

"In your mind," Lynn said with a soft laugh. She carefully painted her lips black while looking in her round compact mirror.

"Listen, zombie-girl," Adam said, trying to get to his feet but failing miserably. He rolled off the beanbag onto the dusty concrete, and wallowed a few moments before finally pushing himself to his feet.

Marty, Dee, and Lynn burst into laughter. Adam sheepishly grinned.

"Careful," Lynn said, holding her purse. "I'm carrying glitter, so if you don't want to be shiny like you were on Halloween, you best calm down."

Adam leaned down and wiped dust off his knees and shorts. He eyed her purse momentarily and then his eyes met her serious gaze. He shook his head. "No thanks. *No* more glitter. That stuff sticks to you worse than sand on a beach."

"But it shows up great on your tanned skin," Lynn said. "Kinda like that greasy dust you're wearing now."

"At least I'm not pale as a—"

Dee rapped the mallet against the podium. "Enough, guys! Sheesh, we should be celebrating! Or, if nothing else, find another mystery and start a new investigation."

Adam groaned.

"What?" Dee said, frowning at him.

"Only if it doesn't involve walking door-to-door again or biking up any more steep hills."

"What are the odds of that?" Lynn said.

Marty cleared his throat. "What type of mystery now, Sis? We haven't heard of anything unusual going on."

Dee smiled. "But *you* can see ghosts. So, let's go to an old spooky abandoned house or a graveyard to use your talent to see if we can help others like we did Sara and Josephine."

"I'm not hunting ghosts," Marty said. "It *isn't* a talent."

"Marty's Ghost Hunters," Adam said. "We could change the club's name to that!"

Dee slammed the mallet down hard and glared. "We *already* have a name for the club."

Adam's eyes widened. He held his hands up in surrender. "I'm joking, sheesh."

A car pulled up outside the closed garage doors. The engine shut off. A car door opened and closed.

"Who's here?" Marty asked.

"I'll see," Dee said, setting the mallet on the workbench and heading to the side garage door. She peered out the window for a moment and turned to Lynn. "It's your mother."

Lynn frowned. "She doesn't get off work for several more hours."

Dee shrugged. "She has today."

Lynn slid off the tool table. Before she turned the garage doorknob, her mother went through the front door. "Hmm. That's strange."

Dee nodded. "Care for some ice tea?"

"I'm not particularly thirsty," Lynn replied.

Dee grinned and her eyebrows rose. "Me, either, *but* it gives us an excuse to go inside and eavesdrop."

"Sneaky," Lynn said, smiling. "I like that."

"Come on," Dee whispered.

CHAPTER 2

Dee and Lynn opened the door that led into the kitchen, peeked inside, and then walked to the refrigerator. Marty and Adam weren't far behind.

"Hi, guys!" Lynn's mother, Glenda, said with a broad smile. She wore a gray pinstripe pantsuit. Her permed brown hair was pinned back with a silver clip. Unlike Lynn, Glenda wore beige and more natural colors. The contrasting differences between her and Lynn's emo appearance made it difficult to picture them as mother and daughter.

"Hey, Mrs. Wilks," Marty said.

Marty and Dee's mother, Terri, walked into the kitchen. She was dressed in a lavender pantsuit, and like Dee, her reddish hair was bobbed at the shoulders. Dee and Terri looked so much alike, a lot of people often asked if they were sisters.

"Mom, *when* did you get home?" Dee asked. "I never heard you pull up in the drive."

"About a half hour ago." She offered a youthful smile. "Dee, Marty, both of you need to pack enough clothes for the next three days."

Dee gave a curious frown. "Why?"

"Yeah, Mom," Marty said. "Why?"

"You, too, Lynn," Glenda said.

"What?" Lynn said, looking perplexed.

Terri glanced at Glenda and then back to the children. The two women beamed wide smiles. "Our boss booked us for a business training seminar at Morgan's Cove. We might as well let the rest of you enjoy it as a summer vacation!"

Lynn and Dee faced each other, joined hands, and squealed.

"Yeah!" Marty said, shaking his fist in the air.

Sadness claimed Adam's face.

"Oh, don't pout, Adam," Terri said. "I called your mother and she said that it's perfectly fine if you want to go with us. In fact, she's packing your suitcase right now."

"Want to? Yeah!" Adam said with an even broader grin than the rest of the Mystery Solvers. He high-fived Marty.

"Guys," Terri said. "Don't forget swim trunks. There's a pool at the hotel or the beach if you want to see the ocean."

Dee hugged Lynn fiercely. "This is going to be so-o-o cool."

"Yep," Lynn said, trying to loosen Dee's embrace.

Dee turned toward her mother. "Three whole days at the beach? Really?"

"Yes, dear. Now, go pack your suitcase. You too, Marty."

"Come on, Lynn," Glenda said. "We've got to get our things together, too."

"When are we leaving?" Marty asked.

"We have to be on the road this evening," Terri said. "It takes a little over two hours to get to Morgan's Cove. Our first seminar is at 8 a.m., so I'd rather drive tonight instead of getting up at five o'clock in the morning."

"That'd be too early," Dee said.

"Breakfast is at 6 a.m., just so you know."

Lynn turned at the door and faced Dee. "See you in a little while. We're going to the beach!"

Adam laughed. "Better bring a gallon of sunscreen to protect your ghostly white skin."

Lynn frowned, crossed her arms, and headed out the door with her mother.

. . .

ABOUT A HALF HOUR LATER, they were loaded into the Sullivan SUV, which seated seven. Terri drove and Glenda sat in the passenger seat. Dee and Lynn sat in the center seat while Marty and Adam rode in the backseat. All the suitcases were neatly lined in the rear cargo area.

Terri looked in the rearview mirror and smiled. "Congratulations on getting your names into the newspaper, guys."

Dee blushed and glanced at Lynn. "Uh, thanks, Mom."

"You know, you and Marty will be having a serious talk with your father and I once we get back home. We'd have already talked except he's out of town on business. He'll be home when we return. Just so you know."

"And that goes for you, too, Missy," Glenda said, turning to face Lynn.

"Yes, ma'am," the three replied in glum unison.

Dee sighed. "Grandpa already gave me a good chewing."

"He knew you went into Tangled Forest?" Terri asked.

"Yeah."

"I suppose he'll be sitting in on this family meeting with the two of you," Terri said firmly. "I can't believe he didn't tell us. That forest's known for its dangers far longer than I've been alive."

"Yes, mother," Dee said.

Terri glanced at Glenda. "Sometimes I think their Grandpa is a bigger kid than the children."

"Yes, but at least you have him. My father died several years ago."

"That's true. He tries my patience with the best of them, but life would be boring without him," Terri replied with a slight smile. Then she eyed Dee in the mirror for a moment and nodded. "Okay, let's not get into all that right now. No sense weighting down an otherwise relaxing time. Meantime, let's enjoy our time at the beach."

Glenda laughed. "They can enjoy it, but not us. More boring lectures on client motivation. You kids make sure you have enough fun for Terri and myself. Heaven knows, we're going to be bored out of our minds."

"Ain't that the truth," Terri said softly.

"I can't wait," Lynn whispered to Dee. "The ocean waves, sandy beach, and you know what? I want to find a conch shell."

"Oh!" Adam said, leaning forward against his seatbelt strap. "Aren't those the ones you can use for a horn?"

Lynn nodded and grinned while looking over her shoulder.

"That would be nice, but they're hard to find," Dee said.

"What I'd like is to find buried treasure," Adam said, briskly rubbing his hands together.

"Who wouldn't?" Lynn said, laughing.

"Arrgh," Adam said, closing one eye and snarling. "Loot me some pirate's gold."

"Keep dreaming," Dee said.

Marty flipped a page on his smartphone. "Actually, Sis, Morgan's Cove was a popular spot for pirates in the 1700s. It's possible to find treasure long buried and forgotten."

Dee turned sideways, facing Lynn and where she could see Marty and Adam in the backseat. "Well, that's true. Maybe you could find a ghost who could point the way for us?"

"Shh!" Marty frowned and put his finger to his lips.

"Sorry," she whispered.

Lynn brought up information for Morgan's Cove on her phone. "There are some haunted places in the city. Mainly tourists attractions, so they might not be real ghosts."

"Marty will scour the streets for us," Dee said.

"I will *not*."

Re-o-o-w!

"Edgar?" Terri asked, glancing into the mirror. "Who brought the cat?"

"None of us brought *Pyewackett*," Dee said, trying to hide the cat between herself and Lynn.

Pyewackett purred loudly.

"I hear him," Terri said.

"Yes, but erm, we didn't bring him. I guess he stowed away," Dee replied, nervously glancing at Marty.

Her mother groaned. "I don't have time to turn around and take him home, so you'd best keep a close eye on him. If you lose him in Morgan's Cove, there's nothing we can do."

Marty leaned over the seat and took the cat. "We'll keep him with us at all times."

"Unlikely," Dee whispered. "He comes and goes as he pleases."

"Who decided to change your cat's name?" Terri asked.

The four Mystery Solvers exchanged glances. Dee quickly spoke up. "It was a club decision, Mom."

"Why?"

"Because Edgar … sounds so old," Dee replied.

Glenda turned in her seat and looked over her shoulder. "Pyewackett isn't old? It isn't a name you hear except when it's connected to witches."

"Really?" Dee asked with a feigned look of surprise. "I think it has a *mystery* element to it. Dark and mysterious. Don't you agree?"

"If you say so," Terri said, glancing at her daughter in the rearview mirror. "Just make sure you keep a close eye on him so he doesn't dart off when we get to the hotel."

"We will," Marty said, scratching behind the cat's ears.

CHAPTER 3

The harsh beeping of the alarm clock caused Dee to jump up and swing her legs over the side of the bed. She rubbed her eyes and for several seconds, she looked around, unable to place where she was.

Her mother shut off the alarm. "It's still early, Dee. You don't have to get up yet. I can wake you after I've showered and gotten ready."

Dee yawned, stretched, and rubbed her eyes. "After that startling alarm? I doubt I can go back to sleep."

"Okay, I'll take a quick shower and get dressed for my morning meeting. After that, the shower's yours. I doubt Marty or Adam have even woke up after their alarm."

"Glenda will wake them though, right?" Dee asked.

"Yes. See what's on television—"

Dee picked up her cellphone and began scrolling through "Places to See in Morgan's Cove" on her phone, oblivious of anything else.

Terri shook her head. "These days, no television for kids your age, huh? Always the cellphones, right, Dee?"

Dee didn't acknowledge the questions.

Terri frowned. "*Dee!*"

Dee jerked slightly and she shrugged. "It's faster to find information. Besides, nothing interests me on television."

Terri sighed. "While you're scanning information, how about checking the weather? You might also check the times of the tides for when the four of you head to the beach."

"Sure thing, Mom. Thanks for bringing us, by the way," she said without glancing away from the phone.

Terri laughed. "Can't leave you at home since your Dad's out of town."

"You could've left us with Grandpa."

"No-o-o. He's in the doghouse right now."

Dee looked away from her phone with genuine sadness. "Aw, for real, Mom? He was only looking out for us in his own way."

"Yeah, to keep that information away from us, and while I understand he doesn't want you punished, he definitely needs to let your father and I know when you've done something foolish."

Her mother closed the bathroom door. A few seconds later, the shower came on. Dee glanced at Lynn, who was asleep and hugging her pillow tightly. Lynn's alabaster skin reminded Dee of an antique porcelain doll or photos she'd seen of Geisha girls. Of course, with the dark mascara, Lynn often looked ready to mime at a carnival or mimic the undead in a zombie show. She wondered why Lynn preferred staying pale when so many others spent hours in the sun or at a tanning bed, trying to get the perfect tan. Dee admired Lynn for being herself, even if she was far different than everyone else. That took courage, which made Dee proud to have Lynn as her friend and a fellow club member.

Dee scanned a weather website for the temperature and the times of the high and low tides. Then she returned to the local tourist attractions, particularly those with the claim of being haunted.

For as long as she could remember, Dee always wanted to see a ghost; mainly due to others saying they'd seen ghosts. Those who saw ghosts often didn't tell others because people stood in opposition, insisting that ghosts didn't exist. But now, thanks to Pyewackett, she had seen several ghosts. However, Marty kept his blessing of having the ability to see them. She didn't understand why Marty viewed his talent as an affliction. She'd swap places with him in a heartbeat, just to be able to see them. He didn't understand how lucky he was.

Lynn stirred beneath her blankets and lazily opened one eye to stare at Dee. "What time is it?"

"Fifteen minutes until six."

She groaned and pulled the blanket over her head. "Seriously?"

"Yep. Mom's in the shower. Your mother's probably up, too."

"Probably. I think I want to sleep in," Lynn said.

Dee stood, jumped, and flung herself backwards to land hard on the bed, causing Lynn to bounce on the mattress.

"Hey!" Lynn said, frowning. "Beauty rest here, okay?"

"Oh, really? And what if I bounce you right out of—"

Lynn popped Dee in the face with her pillow.

"Ah, well, that does it!" Dee grabbed her pillow and swung hard at Lynn.

Lynn rolled from the bed, dodging the strike, and parried with her pillow. They kept flinging their pillows at one another and successfully blocking each potential blow while giggling loudly.

"You're awake now," Dee said.

"Yep."

The shower water stopped and the curtain hooks scraped the bar with a squeal. "What are you girls doing?"

"Pillow fight, Mom."

"Don't break anything or it comes out of your allowance."

Dee cocked a brow and gave a mischievous grin at Lynn. "Truce?"

"Sure. Besides, I want to see the sunrise over the ocean."

Dee nodded and tossed her pillow onto the messy bed. Lynn swung hard, popping Dee's face.

"Hey!"

"I win!" Lynn said.

"Sneaky and underhanded."

Lynn shrugged. "You're a lot tougher than I am, so I have to improvise."

"You know I owe you one," Dee said with a sneer and pointing her finger.

Terri opened the bathroom door. Clouds of steam drifted out. "Decide which of you showers first and hurry up. We all need to eat breakfast."

CHAPTER 4

After everyone showered and dressed, they met at the hotel buffet dining room and ate.

Terri stood with her empty plate, glanced at her watch, and said, "Glenda and I need to go sign in and get our badges for the sales meeting. The four of you are to be on your best behavior. Is that understood?"

The Mystery Solvers all nodded.

"Good. Like I mentioned yesterday evening, we're all going to discuss the Tangled Forest incident. If you'd like a bit of leniency, prove yourselves to us during the next three days by showing some responsibility," Terri said. "And be careful. Make sure you only swim where lifeguards are on duty."

Glenda's dimples deepened as she smiled and nodded. "Our seminar classes end at five o'clock, so Lynn, I expect you back at the room by then, okay?"

"Sure."

"That goes for all of you," Terri said. "And Dee?"

"Yes, mother?"

"Marty's in charge, just so you know."

Dee rolled her eyes and groaned. "Oh, all right."

"Marty," Terri said. "Since you're the oldest, I expect you to keep them on their best behavior. If Dee gives you any lip, let me know. I'll deal with her after the seminar's over."

"Oka-a-ay, mother," Dee said. "I'll do what he says, okay? Now, you two be good adults and hurry along so you're not late for the seminar."

Terri rested her hands on her hips and frowned. Her jaw tightened and she opened her mouth to speak. Dee grinned and waved her hands in surrender.

"Kidding, mother. I'm only kidding," Dee said.

"Dee, *don't* get sassy with me. You're in enough trouble as it is by going to Tangled Forest without adult supervision. I'm in no mood this morning, okay?"

Dee's grin faded. She swallowed hard and looked down. "I'm sorry. Really, I am. I was only playing."

Her mother leaned down to kiss her cheek and then whispered, "I know you're just trying to show out in front of your friends, but now's not the time."

"Yes, Mom."

Terri grabbed her suede satchel purse and slid it over her shoulder. "Remember, 5 p.m. sharp."

The Mystery Solvers all nodded.

DEE WAS quiet after the two mothers left to attend the conference. Humbled and embarrassed was a better way to describe her sudden silence. She took her cellphone and sat at the small round table at the corner of the hotel room, pouting. Her lower lip vibrated slightly, and it appeared she might burst into tears at any moment.

Marty grabbed his phone and tucked it into a side pocket of his cargo shorts. "I know it's early, but let's not waste our time inside when we have the beach and lots of places to explore. Dee, you have one of those haunted places picked out?"

Still glum, Dee shrugged. "They don't open until nine."

"There's other things we can do," Marty said, trying to shake Dee from her glumness. "Let's vote as to what we should do first."

"I have a suggestion," Lynn said.

"Great," Marty said. "What?"

"Can we go to the beach first?"

Dee turned and gave Lynn a side-glance. "Why?"

"According to the weather site, the morning tide's receding. That's the best time to find conch shells, before a lot of people comb the beach. I really want one. It'd be more meaningful if I found one instead of buying one."

"Sure," Marty said. "If we hurry, we might find you one."

CHAPTER 5

In less than ten minutes, the Mystery Solvers walked across the sand dunes to the saturated shoreline. Their flip-flops made strange wet sucking sounds. Cold shallow waves washed across their feet and receded. Seagulls lofted in the air, hoping for early morning handouts of bread or popcorn, neither of which the Mystery Solvers carried. Twice, startled fiddler crabs kicked up sand near the sand dunes. The crabs danced sideways, snapping their pinchers defensively before scuttling away.

The cool ocean breeze bent rows of sea oats into a strange dancing routine. The salty spray off the white-capped waves coated everything along the shoreline with moisture.

"Look!" Adam said, pointing to the ocean. "Is that a dolphin or porpoise?"

Marty shrugged. "From this distance, it's hard to tell."

"Oh!" Lynn said, taking her smartphone and snapping pictures. "There are several of them."

The hooked dorsal fins broke the water's surface in up and down motions as the dolphins swam in unison. The rising sun looked punctured and bled brilliant orange, yellow, pink, and red colors behind puffy grayish-blue clouds.

Lynn paused from picture-taking and scanned the wet sand for large shells. The ocean breeze tousled her hair. Dee walked several paces behind everyone, still carrying a dampened spirit. Getting scolded was never easy, and it was even worse when it happened in front of one's friends.

Adam glanced at Lynn and asked, "Did you slather yourself up with sunscreen?"

"No. the sun's just now rising. But I will once we get back to the room," she replied.

"You might be burnt toast by then," Adam said.

"You'd like that, wouldn't you?"

"Not particularly, no."

The roaring ocean waves crashed on the beach near their feet. As the water slowly receded, pebbles, broken and perfect shells littered the smooth sand. Where these pieces remained, odd grooved patterns left tracks behind each ornamental object the ocean discarded on the shore. A large, whiter than bone, object was being sucked across the sand toward the frothy rolling waves.

Dee, who continued to be dejected, saw it. "Wow!" She ran after the large sand dollar and held it up. It gleamed bright white.

"Nice find!" Marty said.

"It is, isn't it?" Dee said. Her face beamed a broad smile.

Adam laughed. "It's whiter than Lynn's skin. If she was any brighter skin-toned, she could stand on the shore at night to guide ships instead of a lighthouse."

Lynn's jaw tightened. She huffed and shook her head angrily.

"Ignore him, Lynn," Marty said. He frowned at Adam. "His words simply prove how childish he really is. I think we'd have been better off leaving him in Ravenswood. If his rude attitude continues, I make the nomination to have him removed from our club."

Adam's eyes widened with sudden nervousness. "Chill. I was only joking."

"Well, you've done it enough, okay?" Marty said. "To tease is one thing, but you've picked at her a lot lately and that's bullying."

"Sheesh," Adam said. His brow furrowed. Frantic, he turned to Lynn. "Lynn, I'm sorry. I was kidding. I didn't mean to hurt your feelings."

Lynn shrugged, crossed her arms, and walked along the sand on the other side of Marty. Foamy waves washed across her feet. "Don't worry about it."

"Hey, I'll stop. I promise."

Marty walked alongside Lynn.

"I've not seen any large shells yet," she said, giving a side-glance to Marty. She squinted as the harsh morning sun struck her eyes.

"We've only started looking."

An old man with bright pink skin approached. In passing, they noticed the large conch shell in his left hand.

"Where'd you find that?" Lynn asked.

The man turned, still in stride, and pointed. "Near those large rocks."

"Thanks," Lynn said, but the man kept walking in a hurry.

"Let's go check around those rocky bar," Dee said, admiring her sand dollar.

The jagged rocks formed a dividing wall on the beach and extended out into the ocean for about a hundred yards. Posted signs warned not to swim or surf near the outcrop.

Adam walked beside Marty. "You would really have me removed from the club for teasing Lynn?"

Marty nodded. "Yes. We should be working together as a group and have each other's back."

"But I do."

"Maybe. Maybe not. Constantly picking at her only causes strife and division. We don't need any negativity."

Adam nodded. "I agree. It won't happen again."

Lynn ran ahead of them until she reached the lower edge of the outcrop. Waves sloshed and cascaded against the wall. Several seagulls hovered over the ocean and a few more were perched and pecking at the remains of a crab. Huge pelicans flapped and landed on the jagged stones farther from shore.

She stepped onto the outcrop and held her arms out to her sides to keep balance. She climbed and made her way along the rocks until she was about twenty feet from the shore.

"Be careful," Marty said.

"I will."

Marty picked up his pace. "Wait up, Lynn."

"I found one," Lynn said, kneeling. She cupped her left hand into a rough groove of the rocks and leaned, trying to reach the shell with her right hand. "But it's out of reach."

"Give me a minute and I'll come help you," Marty said.

CHAPTER 6

$\mathcal{M}$arty carefully made his way to where Lynn was stooped. "See it?" she said.

He nodded.

"It's stuck in that pocket of water, but my arms aren't long enough to reach it."

Marty put one hand on her elbow and then placed his other hand atop hers that she held the rock with. "I've got you. Grab my hand. I'll hold on so you can reach the shell, but please be careful. If you fall, the tide could pull you under."

Lynn stood, took his hand, and then stretched down, placing her hand on the shell. "Got it!"

Once she picked it up, Marty pulled her upright and toward him. They stood awkwardly close face-to-face and when their eyes met, they blushed.

"Thanks, Marty," she said with a smile. "I couldn't have ever reached it without your help."

"You're welcome." He glanced at the water where she had grabbed the shell. Something wrapped in thick seaweed bobbed in the ocean near the rocky ledge. "Hey, what's that?"

She turned and noticed the object. "Is that a bottle?"

"It could be, but I can't tell for certain with all that green guck stuck to it," Marty said, lowering himself to the ledge of the rocky barrier. The waves sloshed heavily.

Lynn grabbed the back of his shirt. "Please be careful. If you fall, you'll take me with you. I didn't notice how bad those waves were when I grabbed the shell."

"I'm fine."

"Would you two lovebirds hurry it up?" Dee shouted.

Lynn and Marty exchanged surprised expressions and their faces reddened.

"Lovebirds?" Adam asked, puzzled. "You mean they like each other?"

"Isn't it obvious?" Dee asked.

"That'd explain why he got so mad over me teasing her," Adam said in a near whisper.

"We found something, Dee," Lynn said.

"What?"

Marty groaned and stretched until his fingers grasped the slimy seaweed. A disgusted expression came to his face. He pinched it and pulled the long object onto a rock. "I got it."

He picked the object up and placed it on the rocks beside Lynn. After repositioning himself, he pressed his palms on the rock to pull himself up beside her. Thin cuts on his hands filled with blood. "Dang. These rocks are as sharp as glass."

"I know."

"What is that?" Dee asked.

Marty wiped his bleeding hands on his shorts before picking up the seaweed-covered object and walking to his sister and Adam.

"Ugh," Adam said, scrunching his nose. "That looks nasty."

Dee shook her head. "I can't believe you're touching it."

"I'm not too fond of holding it, but how else are we going to examine it?" Marty knelt on the cool, wet sand and began ripping away the layers of seaweed from the object.

"It *is* a bottle with a cork," Lynn said, dropping to her knees beside him.

"It's a weird looking bottle," Adam said.

Marty pulled the last of the seaweed off the glass. The bottle was long with a smooth opening plugged with an aged black, slimy cork.

"What's inside?" Dee asked, squatting to look closer.

"Some sort of rolled yellow paper," Marty said.

"Wow," Lynn said.

"All right! Open it!" Adam said. "It could be a treasure map."

Everyone else laughed.

"Hey," Adam said, shrugging. "It's entirely possible."

"Only one way to find out," Marty said, pulling at the cork. After a few seconds, he shook his head. "The cork's too swollen to pry loose."

"We need to get it out," Adam said. "Break it open."

"No, we might damage the paper." Marty stood. "We need to get a knife to cut the cork out."

"You need some bandaids," Dee said.

He turned his palms upward and shook his head. "The cuts are shallow and looks like the bleeding has stopped."

"Where can we get a knife?" Adam asked.

"I have a metal hair clasp," Lynn said, digging through her fanny pack. "Here."

Marty took the clasp and unfastened it. He studied the clasp for a few moments. "It might get broken."

She shrugged. "It's an old one, so go ahead."

He walked to a bench along the boardwalk and sat down. The others joined him. Taking the sharp tip, he jabbed it into the top of the swollen cork. Water leaked from the pores. With a little bit of pressure he pried a chunk out. The remainder of the cork broke into pieces.

"I don't see how this cork has survived so long. It's practically rotten," Marty said.

"That means the bottle's old," Dee said.

Marty nodded and pulled out the split cork, careful not to allow any water to seep through the bottle's opening and damage the paper. He handed the hair clasp back to Lynn. "Thanks."

Lynn smiled and slid the clasp into her pack. Then she handed her conch shell for Dee to examine.

Marty took the end of his shirt and dried the top of the bottle, then he tipped it and allowed the rolled parchment to slide out. He gave everyone a serious stare. Their eyes were wide with excitement. "Guys, you know this could be someone's practical joke."

"Perhaps *ages* ago. It's doubtful anyone could have done this recently," Dee said, rubbing her hands together. "But either way, it might be our next mystery to solve."

Marty unrolled the yellow parchment. The black ink had faded over time, but it was still readable. A map. A large black X was marked with a winding broken dotted line, possibly indicating the path one needed to take to find whatever was hidden, which might or might *not* lead to treasure.

"It *is* a map!" Adam said. "I knew it!"

Dee pointed at the corner of the map. "1835. You think this is the actual date of the map?"

Marty shrugged. "It might be, if the map's authentic."

"It certainly looks authentic," Dee said.

"I agree, but unless we actually have someone date it, we're still only guessing." He picked up the bottle and examined it. On the bottom was what looked like the initials of a company with 1822 indented into the glass. "The bottle looks genuine."

"How'd it keep from getting broken for all these years?" Lynn asked.

"The wrapped seaweed must have cushioned it," Marty replied.

"Let's take it back to the hotel," Dee said. "Maybe we could take the bottle to some of the tourist shops and see if anyone knows what the bottle once held inside *besides* the map."

Adam shook his head. "Don't tell them about the map though."

"Of course not, silly," Dee said. "That's *our* mystery to solve, provided we find any information that supports our theory of the bottle actually being from the early 1800s."

"I need to go 'slather a gallon of sunscreen on' anyways," Lynn said, giving Adam a sharp look.

Adam blushed but didn't say anything.

Marty checked the time on his phone. "By the time we go to the room and hide the map, some of the local shops should be open."

CHAPTER 7

After applying fresh coats of sunscreen at the hotel room, the four Mystery Solvers sat at the round table in the corner. With nervous fingers, Marty took the map and unrolled it, using several heavy items and Lynn's conch shell to hold down the corners to prevent it from rolling up again. The heavy paper was rough to the touch and tattered around the edges.

Near the center of the map was a large X. Only a few places on the map were easy to identify based on their geographic location. The biggest was the bay area and the long rock wall where they had discovered the map and the shell. A broken ship with a pirate's flag was drawn near the rocks.

"What does that mean?" Dee asked, pointing at the shipwreck image.

"Hard to do more than guess right now," Marty replied. "Whoever drew this map might have been aboard a ship that wrecked or might've found the wrecked ship and took the treasure to hide it. Or, this map was made by a pirate who owned the ship or by someone who stumbled upon the ship. Or there wasn't a shipwreck at all. Perhaps it was a warning about the rocks?"

"That's a lot of guessing," Adam said.

"It all adds to the mystery," Dee said with a grin.

Marty nodded. "Definitely."

Since they were visiting Morgan's Cove for the first time, they knew relatively little of the city's history. Reading a map like this was similar to reading a foreign language. Without knowing the landmarks or the area's history, all they could do was stare at the map with studious frowns. Occasionally, they gave one another confused looks, and each seemed to be waiting for the other to speak.

Finally, Marty said, "I imagine this entire area has drastically changed since when the map was drawn. None of the places on this map will be easily located, if any can be found at all."

"Then what do we do?" Lynn asked.

Adam nodded. "Yeah. We *need* to find this treasure."

"The treasure might not even exist or someone might have already found it," Marty said. "But if it does exist and no one's found it, there's a good chance we can find more information."

"Actually, Marty," Dee said, looking at her smartphone screen. "One of the local museums, Pirate Jack's Treasure Box, sells local treasure maps."

"Really?" Adam asked. "For genuine treasure or make believe?"

Marty stood. "Only one way to find out. Let's go check it out." He handed Lynn her conch shell, rolled up the map, and tucked it inside his suitcase under the bed. Then he grabbed the old bottle and walked to the door.

"What are you going to do with that?" Adam asked.

"See if anyone has any idea as to how old it is," he replied.

"You think anyone would know?" Dee asked.

Marty shrugged. "People collect all sorts of old bottles and other objects. Probably a few antique stores here."

CHAPTER 8

The four Mystery Solvers walked down the boardwalk along the edge of the beach. More people combed the beach hunting and picking up shells. An old scruffy man with gray sideburns and a wiry beard wore a pirate-tied bandana. His left eye was covered with a black patch. Shirtless and wearing flip-flops, he stood in the sand with a metal detector. His skin was dark tan and almost leathery, which made it difficult to tell if his wrinkles were from age or from too many hours in the sun. His thin frame was slightly stooped. His ribs were visible but his stomach pooched slightly.

The old man moved the metal detector back and forth across the sand. Since he wore headphones, the machine made no audible sounds.

Marty and the other Mystery Solvers stopped to watch for a moment. As if the old man felt their stares, he paused and glanced up. His one eye was a brilliant icy blue and unnerving as it narrowed while he studied them.

"Can I help you lads?" he asked, sliding the headphones off his ears and letting them rest on his shoulders.

"No, sir," Marty replied. "Just watching to see if you find anything. I've always wanted to use a metal detector."

The man chuckled and grinned, making the wrinkles on his face more prominent.

"Have you found anything?" Dee asked.

"This morning? No," he replied in a tired voice, shaking his head. "But it's still early."

Adam stepped closer and examined the metal detector. "Have you *ever* found anything valuable?"

The old man rubbed his scruffy chin. "Depends upon what you consider *valuable*. On occasion, I've found wedding rings, class rings, necklaces, and such. Quarters, dimes, pennies. It adds up over time."

"That's cool, but I mean like gold or silver. Treasure," Adam said with raised brows.

"No-o-o. If I had, do you think I'd still be doing this?" he asked. Then he bellowed a hardy laugh. He glanced at Marty with sudden curiosity. "Where'd you get that old bottle, son?"

"Ah, we found it near those rocks." Marty pointed to the jagged rocks near the beach.

"May I see it?" he asked, extending his hand. His jagged fingernails were cracked and a couple were black.

Marty shrugged slightly and handed it to him. "Sure."

The man held the bottle up and peered through the glass, as if picturing what might have been inside. Then he looked at the bottom of the bottle and ran a thumb across the indented date. His eyes gleamed with excitement. "I'd hang on to that if I were you. It's much older than I am, which means it's *quite* old. Ha-ha. What's these weird patterns on the outside of the glass?"

"It was wrapped in seaweed."

"Interesting."

Marty nodded and accepted the bottle back. "We thought so, too."

"Was there anything in it?" he asked.

Adam opened his mouth, but Marty quickly said, "No. Nothing but air."

"Really?" His eye flicked toward Adam.

Adam's eyes widened at Marty's reply. When the old man's icy blue eye seemed to be cross-examining Adam and reading his body language, Adam nervously glanced at his feet.

"Nothing at all? Hmm, from the looks of the rim, the bottle had a cork. How else could it stay afloat for years?"

"It had a cork," Lynn said.

"But nothing inside?" the man shook his head. "I find that hard to believe. No one corks an empty bottle and tosses it into the ocean."

"Maybe someone already found it before us," Adam said, trying to hide the nervousness in his voice. "And he took whatever was in it?"

"I suppose that's a possibility. But it's really a shame if that's the case," he replied. "Legend has it of a hidden pirate chest here in Morgan's Cove, buried by Peg-leg Jack, but no one's ever found it. Originally, that treasure was the reason I bought this detector. Of course, I was younger and more ambitious, and thought that I'd be the one that finally found the loot. Now that I'm retired, I spend far too many hours on the beach looking for clues. It's become my obsession. A daily ritual. But, no luck yet. It's such a shame you didn't find a map inside that bottle."

Dee smiled. "We were heading to Pirate Jack's shop to buy a map."

The old man chuckled. "Save your money. That map's rubbish."

"You've used it?" Dee asked.

"Me and a million other saps," he said in a low raspy growl. "It's the only treasure they have to offer."

"What do you mean?" Lynn asked.

"They're making a fortune selling those fake maps and sending people out on wild goose chases."

"So you don't think the treasure exists?" Adam asked. His voice hinted sheer disappointment.

"Ah, I never said that. I'm certain Peg-leg's treasure is buried somewhere in Morgan's Cove. A true pirate would've hidden his treasure well. Often too well, I'm afraid."

"I don't understand," Lynn said.

"Well, sometimes, a pirate returned to reclaim his fortune but was unable to find where he buried the treasure."

Adam frowned. "But that's why they made maps, right? So they wouldn't *lose* their treasure."

Ol' Patch chuckled. "That's why they *drew* them, but a lot of other things might have prevented them from finding where they buried it, even though they had a map."

"Like what?" Dee asked.

"The distances from point A to point B might not be accurate, since they often used long strides to number their steps. That's not very accurate, if you think about it."

"I guess not," Adam said.

"If you have a peg-leg and drunk, your steps probably wouldn't be equal. Or they arrived at the wrong place that looked like where they had buried it." He sighed. "Or say the treasure was buried in a grove of palm trees but a blasted hurricane destroyed the coastline and washed the trees out to sea. There are numerous reasons for why a pirate might never reclaim his treasure. Death, though, is probably the number one reason."

Dee smiled. "Those reasons all make sense."

"As I said, it's a shame you didn't find a map in that bottle. Peg-leg's treasure remains a mystery or perhaps it's just a fairytale. But whichever, I best get back to searching for loot. Might find enough change to buy myself some coffee and breakfast later."

Marty nodded and extended his hand. "It was good to meet you."

"Ah, be the same here," he said, shaking Marty's hand. Then he tapped his eye patch gently. "Folks around here call me Ol' Patch. And you kids can feel free to do the same."

"I'm Marty. This is Dee, Lynn, and Adam."

"Welcome to the cove, kids. If it be treasure you hunt, may you have better fortune than I've had over the years. If you need any advice or help, I'm never hard to find. You'll see me somewhere along the shore most hours in the mornings and evenings. I'm too old to endure much of the noon and early afternoon heat. That's when I am hiding in the shade daydreaming." He looked at Lynn and shook his head. "If I were you, I'd stay indoors as much as possible. As pale as you are, you're going to blister fast from the hot sun and the warm breeze."

Lynn nodded and held up her beach bag. "I'm wearing sunscreen and have a long-sleeved shirt and blanket in this. I'm good."

"Glad you came prepared. Good luck in your endeavors, kids. Perhaps our paths will cross again." With that, he smiled, placed the headset over his ears and returned to scoping the surface of the sand with his metal detector.

They smiled and nodded, but his attention had already turned, preventing him from seeing or acknowledging their good-byes, so they continued down the boardwalk.

"He seems nice enough," Lynn said.

"I don't know," Dee said. "He seems a bit … strange."

"You think so, too?" Adam said, swallowing hard.

Dee nodded. "Yeah, he seems a bit shady. Maybe a tad … creepy."

Marty laughed. "Oh, come on. Shady? He's dressed like a pirate and probably playacting to add to the city's lore."

"Sometimes the ones who act the most friendly are the ones you should fear the most," Lynn said.

Marty was silent for a few moments. He nodded. "That's true, too. But he seemed okay to me. Let's go find that shop."

Adam looked over his shoulder. Ol' Patch had taken off his headset and was watching the four Mystery Solvers. He frowned with a tightened jaw and showed his teeth. Adam turned and sped up his pace.

$\mathcal{M}$arty led them off the boardwalk and onto the oceanfront sidewalk where all the shops, restaurants, and museums were located. Some of the shops were just opening, but others wouldn't open for another hour. The busiest places seemed to be the ones selling coffee or breakfast sandwiches.

"Before we return to the hotel," Marty said, "I'd like to go into one of the T-shirt shops."

"Sounds like fun," Dee said. "You didn't find Ol' Patch a bit odd?"

"Not really. He didn't seem threatening."

"I found him a bit creepy," Lynn said.

"Why?" Marty asked.

"It's hard to trust anyone dressed like a wannabe pirate."

Marty laughed.

"He certainly kept his eye on the bottle," Dee said. "No pun intended."

"Yeah," Adam said with a nervous laugh. "The way he was looking at the bottle and us, I have a feeling he knew we were lying about not finding a map."

Marty shrugged. "It doesn't matter what he thinks though. We found the map, it's ours, and since we didn't bring it with us, all he has are his suspicions."

"I have an uneasy feeling that it won't be the last time we see him," Adam said.

"Why's that?" Dee asked.

Adam told them about how Ol' Patch turned around and watched them walking up the boardwalk and the odd face he had made.

"Are you sure?" Lynn asked. "You do tend to get overly nervous ever since we went into Tangled Forest, you know?"

"I'm sure he was watching us," Adam said, frowning.

Lynn glanced at Marty. "Do you think he might come after us to try to steal the map?"

"Since we don't know him, let's not panic and think the worst of him," Marty said. "But, we need to stay alert. If you see him following us, speak up, and let the others know. Just as a precaution. Deal?"

"Deal," Adam said.

Dee and Lynn nodded.

"Let's not ruin our vacation by constant worry," Marty said.

"Hey!" Dee pointed across the street. "There's the pirate shop."

They walked to the pedestrian crossing where a yellow caution light flashed above the center of the street. The morning traffic was sparse, so they were able to cross quickly.

On the side of the building was a mural of a pirate climbing the ropes of a ship's mast with a skull and crossbones flag at the top. The artist had rendered such incredibly accurate 3D images that it almost looked like the pirate would move upwards.

"It gets hot here early, doesn't it?" Marty asked, wiping his brow with his hand.

"Yep," Dee said. She pushed the shop door inward and cool air flowed out around them. "But it's nice inside."

"In that case, I might not want to leave," Marty said.

At first glance, the decor of the room was mostly a lot of open treasure chests filled with various souvenirs: hats, scarves, Jolly Roger flags, fake swords and pistols, and small jewelry boxes shaped like chests. Murals of different pirate captains and their ships with the sea behind them brightened the wall. Written beneath each captain was a short bio and his major thefts on the high seas. Marty found it odd how ruthless pirates had once been feared long ago, but now, most people glamorized pirates as nothing more than a Robin Hood type figure. But Robin Hood never killed the people he robbed.

"Ah, our first customers of the day or are ye trespassers?" said the black-haired woman with curly braids as she stood behind the counter and spoke with a cheery voice. She stepped around toward them, dressed in a leather swashbuckler costume with the pirate hat to boot. She squinted one eye closed as she talked. "Welcome to Pirate Jack's Treasure Box. My name's Mary. Are you here for the tour, lads and lasses, or to browse our souvenirs? Argh ... but I gotta warn ya, we might be pirates, but we don't take kindly to thieves in our establishment."

The four Mystery Solvers laughed.

"We're not thieves," Marty said, grinning.

"We saw online that you sold treasure maps for Morgan's Cove," Dee said with a broad smile.

"That we do, Miss. It's our most popular item," she said, waving her plastic sword and pointing at the small barrel with dozens of rolled, poster-sized maps tucked inside.

"So we've heard," Adam said.

"Oh? From whom?" Mary asked.

"An old man we passed on the beach on our way here."

Mary's brow furrowed but her eyes brimmed with enthusiasm. "That wouldn't happen to be Ol' Patch, now would it?"

Adam nodded.

"I imagine he doesn't speak too highly of our map." She rolled her eyes and waved a dismissive hand into the air, bringing the back of it to her forehead as she tilted her head back. "You simply must ignore that poor misguided soul. It's just how he is. Sourer than a persimmon, he is, but I suppose I'd be that way too if I'd have spent more than thirty years hunting for Peg-leg's hidden treasure."

"Thirty years?" Adam asked, perplexed.

Mary smiled and nodded.

"So the treasure's real?" Dee asked.

"According to legend, the treasure's very real," she said. "But, thousands of people have hunted for it. Since no one's ever found it or *reported* finding it, we can only hope it exists."

"Ol' Patch said that the maps you sell are fake and you're conning the people that buy it," Marty said.

Mary sighed. "I'm afraid his bitterness has gotten the best of him or perhaps his brain is fried from spending too much time outdoors. He casts the blame on everyone because he's been unable to find the treasure."

"If the maps you sell are real, why have so many people bought the map but never found the treasure?" Dee asked.

"The map's nothing more than something to give tourists an adventure. That's clearly written in the disclaimer."

"So it's not the *real* map?"

Mary sheathed her fake sword and crossed her arms, offering a slightly agitated smile. "Again, the map we sell is *only* for an adventure. There are no guarantees. As for its accuracy, let me explain. It's a copy of an old map from the previous museum before it burned when I was a child. The problem with the original map was that it didn't have a North arrow or longitudinal or latitudinal coordinates listed. The map was so vague that only the person who had drawn it would have been able to properly decode it, *if* the person was actually able to remember the correct details. The landmarks were vague, too. So we're selling copies of the map that was in the old museum. It's authentic and not a scam. But it won't ever lead anyone directly to the treasure. It can't because it lacks pertinent details. The only way someone will find that treasure is by pure chance or accidentally. Without a proper map legend, it's anybody's guess. A person would have a better chance of winning the lottery than finding this treasure."

"How much for a map?" Marty asked, reaching into his pocket.

"Two dollars," Mary replied. "But let me remind you, there are no guarantees."

"We understand," Marty said with a smile. "But the adventure's worth a lot more than two dollars."

"That's the spirit!" Mary said with a high-pitched laugh.

"How much is the tour?" Dee asked.

"Two dollars for each ticket."

"So ten dollars total?" Marty said, figuring the amount in his head. He took out a ten dollar bill. "Here."

Mary took the money, punched numbers into the cash register, and then put the money inside. "Now, if you four will follow me, the tales of piracy shall begin."

CHAPTER 10

The Mystery Solvers followed Mary into an adjoining room where the lights dimmed and a line of various stations were set up. Each table had a glassed enclosure of a model pirate ship proposed to have belonged to the mural image of the pirate on the wall behind the station.

One by one, Mary talked about the pirates, their ships, the bounties set on each pirate by England, Spain, and France, what the pirates looted, where treasures were believed to have been hidden, and of course, each pirate's ultimate demise.

The last pirate in the museum display was Peg-leg Jack. His life-story was brief but gave the reasons for why legend told of him coming ashore in Morgan's Cove and burying his treasure before finally surrendering to Captain Morgan's pirates and being ordered to be hanged.

"Peg-leg was probably the least successful pirate during his lifetime," Mary said. "But he was also the most hated by Captain Morgan, which explains why Jack was hanged. Captain Morgan was a ruthless man. His only weakness, it seemed, was his various superstitions. And that, dear children, is the last of the tour. I hope you found it entertaining and educational."

"Thanks for such a wonderful tour," Dee said.

"You're most welcome," Mary replied. Then she looked at the bottle in Marty's hand. "I've been wanting to ask *where* you found that bottle? Did you buy it at another shop before you came here?"

Marty shook his head. "No. We found it near the beach."

Mary's eyes widened. "Today?"

"Yes. A few hours ago."

"May I?" she asked, extending her hand toward the bottle.

Marty nodded and handed the bottle to her.

"My gracious," she said.

"What is it?" Dee asked.

"Finding a bottle like this in the ocean after all this time is unheard of," Mary said. She marveled at the bottle, slowly running her fingers over it. "Others like this have been found in Morgan's Cove but usually in places where archaeologists are digging. Was there anything in it? I mean, it had to have been corked or it would have sunk to the bottom of the ocean ages ago."

"Do you think this might have been around during Peg-leg's time?" Marty asked, avoiding her question.

"Yes. We have a couple of bottles similar to this in our personal collection," Mary replied. "They're in that glass case over there, next to our jewelry. Our bottles were unearthed where new buildings were being erected."

The bell attached to the shop's door jangled.

"Jonathan!" Mary said. "Come see what these kids brought in."

Jonathan was slim with tanned skin and in his mid-twenties. He wore a large golden earring in his left ear. His black hair spiraled down in a long ponytail, and like Ol' Patch, he wore a pirate bandana. His black beard was trimmed short. He staggered across the room like a drunken pirate and swaggered flamboyant hand gestures as he spoke in a poor impersonation of Disney's Jack Sparrow. "What did these children bring? Did ye discover something of keen interest?"

Mary handed Jonathan the bottle.

"Well, lookie here," he said, squinting at the bottle under the overhead fluorescent lighting. "Imagine that. Where did you happen upon this?"

"They found it in the ocean this morning," Mary said.

Jonathan stiffened, cocked a brow, and quickly spun toward Marty, breathing in his face. "Did ye now?"

The man's breath was awful, causing Marty's face to scrunch in disgust. He turned his head. Perhaps he *wasn't* pretending to be drunk.

"And what be tucked away inside when you found it?" Jonathan asked, slurring his words.

"Nothing," Marty said, coughing and trying to regain his composure.

"Ah, now, lad, don't be lying to me," Jonathan said in a low angry tone. "Or I might have to find ways to make ye talk."

Marty's eyes widened as did the other three Mystery Solvers when the pirate wannabe's hand rested on the hilt of his dagger.

"What makes you think I'm lying?" Marty asked.

Jonathan laughed, staggered slightly, and offered a shrewd grin. "The fact you ask that question exposes your guilt. But even so, if you look at the bottle in the light, you can see an outline of a scroll from where decades of sun exposure imprinted its image into the glass. So, lad, what did ye find?"

Marty swallowed hard. "Nothing."

Rage claimed the man's face, he grabbed Marty's wrist tightly and pulled him closer. Marty tried to pull free but the man was too strong. The man gritted his teeth and seethed. "Where's the map? Give it to me."

For a moment, Marty thought the man was simply playing the part of a bad pirate, but the dark glint in the man's eyes indicated otherwise. If the man was simply jesting, Marty figured he would've loosened his hold after a few seconds. Instead, he gripped Marty's wrist tighter until it hurt even more. The man was serious.

"Jonathan!" Mary said. "What's gotten into you? That's enough! Let him go right *now!*"

Her tone jarred Jonathan. He shook his head, realized what he was doing, and released Marty, taking a few steps backwards. Marty yanked the bottle from Jonathan's hand and moved to stand between the man and the other three Mystery Solvers.

"My apologies for my brother's unruly behavior." Mary looked at

Jonathan and in a scolding tone, she said, "Seems he's been hitting the bottle of rum a bit early this morning."

"They have the map, Mary," Jonathan said, staggering toward her, slurring his words in a near whisper. "The *real* map. The one we've been looking for all our lives."

"I don't care what they have. It's theirs, if they found it. Go upstairs and sleep it off, John," she said. "Clearly, you're delusional and the liquor's messed with your mind."

"No, sister, they have the map. You mustn't allow them to leave. Not until they give it to us. What they have could be worth millions."

Marty glanced at Dee, Lynn, and Adam. "It's time we get out of here."

The four hurried to the door.

Jonathan growled. "Come back here!"

Marty flung open the door, causing the attached bell to fly across the room and hit the floor. "Go!"

The four fled from the store and ran down the street. When they glanced back, Jonathan stood bent over against the open door, glaring at them. "I'll find you! You'll give us that map!"

CHAPTER 11

The Mystery Solvers ran two blocks before turning into an alley, and then cutting back toward the boardwalk. When Marty thought they had run far enough, he stopped and turned around. He half expected to see Jonathan pursuing them, but then again, the man seemed too drunk to run.

He read the fear in the others' eyes. They leaned against the wall and took deep breaths.

Panting, Marty leaned over. "I think he stopped chasing us."

"Was all of that real?" Dee asked, breathing hard. Her wide eyes remained focused on the alleyway as though she thought the man might appear. "Or was he in character?"

"He was drunk," Marty replied. "I smelled alcohol on his breath. You know, Dee, like Uncle Will?"

Dee faked gagging and then she crinkled her nose. "That bad, huh?"

Marty nodded. "Worse, actually."

Lynn held out her smart phone. "I recorded the whole thing, Marty."

She muted the sound and hit the playback button. The four watched the confrontation on her phone's screen.

"He put his hand on his knife?" Dee asked. "I didn't notice that until now."

"I did," Marty said. "Believe me. No ghost has ever frightened me more than he did, especially when I thought he might pull the knife. Don't delete that, Lynn."

"I won't."

"If he does come after us, we might need to show that to the police," Marty said.

"Maybe we should now?" Lynn asked.

Marty shook his head, still trying to catch his breath. "Not yet. The knife might only be a stage prop he uses for his costume. While it looks convincing enough, there's no sense drawing more attention to ourselves."

"What do you mean?" Dee asked.

"Well, he's really drunk, and after he sleeps it off, maybe he'll forget he met us. But if the police show up and start questioning him … it will arouse his anger again, and then I'm certain he'll try to find us."

Dee nodded. "You're right. The knife might not be real, but he and Ol' Patch both acted certain something was in the bottle."

"I know," Marty said.

Adam was almost as pale as Lynn, but his ashen appearance was due to his fear. He lifted the bill of his cap and wiped sweat from his brow with the back of his hand. "You know what all of this means, right?"

"What?" Lynn asked.

"Our map's real. He went berserk, so it has to be real."

"I agree, Adam," Marty said. "Which means we might be in danger."

"You really think so?" Lynn asked.

"It's valuable. From his reaction, he might use violence to steal it from us," Marty replied. "They talked about how warped Ol' Patch is, but it's obvious Jonathan holds a deeper obsession to get ahold of the map."

"What should we do then?" Adam asked.

Dee frowned. "Let's go back to the hotel room before he sees us. At least we'll be safer there."

"Agreed," Marty said.

They walked at a brisk pace still trying to regain composure after their run. Marty warily kept watch over his shoulder as they hurried down the boardwalk.

"You think we'll have to hide the entire time we're in Morgan's Cove?" Adam asked.

"I don't plan to," Dee said.

"Me, either," Marty said. "But we must stay alert whenever we're not in the hotel. At no time should we get separated from one another. The more people we have around us, the safer we are, especially when we have the map on us."

"You plan to take the map outside the hotel?" Adam asked.

"How else are we going to find what's hidden?" Lynn asked.

"Commit the map to memory?" Adam asked.

Lynn's eyes narrowed as she glanced toward him. "Seriously?"

"Are you saying I'm too stupid to do that?"

"No-o-o," Lynn replied. "Even if you could memorize its pattern, the map has no recent landmarks that make it useful. With the map in hand, at least we'd have a better chance of narrowing down a general area to find the treasure."

Adam frowned. "And having the map on us is a sure way of getting—"

"Shh!" Marty stopped walking and placed a finger to his lips.

"What is it?" Dee whispered.

"Look," Marty pointed. "It's Ol' Patch."

Ol' Patch was searching the sand with his metal detector near the hotel where they were staying. His back was to them, so he hadn't notice their approach.

"What should we do?" Dee asked. "We can't let him know which hotel we're staying at."

"This way," Marty said, walking off the boardwalk and through the outside patio tables at the hotel restaurant.

They hurried past a man sweeping trash into a lobby dustpan. The man never seemed to notice their intrusion and continued sweeping, while listening to music through his earbuds and bopping his head side-to-side.

Marty glanced back after they were on the sidewalk that ran alongside the lower hotel floor. Ol' Patch was still combing the sand, unaware of their proximity. Marty smiled and jogged down the sidewalk with Dee and the others hurrying close behind. They entered the lobby door and headed to the elevator.

After pushing the elevator button, Marty sighed. "So far so good."

"Got my morning exercise," Adam said, panting.

"Be glad it wasn't uphill on a bicycle," Lynn said with a grin.

"You better believe it," he replied, not catching her sarcasm. "I'm not in the mood for that kind of exercise."

The elevator opened and they rushed through the doors. Marty pushed the third floor button several times, hoping the doors closed faster. Although he felt certain no one was actually following them, a part of him feared he might have to fight to protect the others. Since he'd never fought anyone, he worried he wouldn't be able to defend himself well enough to keep the others safe.

Once they were safely inside the hotel room, Marty retrieved the map from the suitcase and brought it to the table. After unrolling it, he said, "Where's the map we got at the pirate shop?"

Dee brought it and handed it to her brother. Marty unrolled it.

"Interesting," he said.

"What?" Dee asked.

Marty placed his finger on the map. "The old map does have a North arrow, but Mary said the map they copied from the old one in the museum didn't. Not that it really matters because there's only one area where those rocks form a wall that run into the ocean. The neat thing is that their new map shows where all the shops, hotels, and restaurants are."

"So?" Adam said, frowning.

"The old map *is* vague. But notice the X on their map isn't in the same place on this old map." Marty grinned.

"Do you think that's on purpose?" Dee asked.

Marty shrugged. "Could be, I suppose. Or, maybe someone made the new map based on their memory of what the old map was supposed to look like."

"See?" Lynn said, looking at Adam.

"What?" he asked.

"Memories can become distorted."

Adam huffed.

"Either way," Marty said, "the reason they want this map so badly is because it shows the real spot where the treasure was buried."

Dee grinned. "So they've been hunting in the wrong place all along?"

"That'd be my guess," Marty replied.

"So what do we do now?" Lynn asked.

Dee placed her finger on the X of the real map. "Let's find out where this spot really is."

CHAPTER 12

Marty placed the old map atop the one they had purchased from the pirate shop. He found it odd the sizes of the maps lined up, and several major key points on the maps did as well. He thought it might be more than coincidence except the map they found had been inside the old bottle. "Wow, would you look at that."

"What?" Adam asked, stepping closer.

"The X on the old map is halfway across town from the fake map."

Dee nodded. "I still wonder if they intentionally made a different location for the X on their map. Because if you think about it, they don't want anyone to actually *find* the treasure. They'd want to send treasure hunters off the trail."

"True," Marty said.

"And all the while, they'd keep making money off the map while they look in the place they suspect the most," Adam said.

"Exactly."

"Then the real question is where have they been searching for the treasure?" Lynn asked.

"Beats me," Marty said.

Dee frowned. "Mary said that they had bottles like ours from the places where archaeologists had dug. Perhaps they're the archaeologists they're referring to?" She looked at the others. They all shrugged. She rubbed her hands together. "Sounds like another mystery."

"What are you implying?" Marty asked. "You think we should spy on them?"

Dee nodded. "Why not?"

"Sis, that's far too dangerous. Why don't you watch the video again where he grabbed me and looked like he might stab me."

"The knife might not have been a real knife," Dee said.

"Are you willing for us to risk the chance that it might be real? I'm not."

"I'm just saying that it'd be good to know *where* they're searching. Besides, spying requires that we not be seen. The art of invisibility."

"Dee, let's just stick to one mystery at a time," Marty said. "We have this old map and know where on the new map we should look."

"I know. But these mysteries are connected and what if they're already digging at that spot? Don't you think it'd be more dangerous if we went there and they're already there?"

"She has a point," Adam said, nervously.

"Let's compare where the X is on the new map to the old one?" Lynn asked.

Marty slid the old map down, so they could read the street names and businesses on the new map. "Mordum's Cemetery." He placed the new map over the old one and carefully marked a faint X onto the map he bought.

"Okay, big brother," Dee said, "if you don't want to spy on Mary and Jonathan, we could take a cab or bus out to the cemetery. It's highly unlikely we'd encounter them there. You can't legally dig in a cemetery unless you're a gravedigger."

Marty shrugged. "Perhaps not in the open or during daylight."

Adam swallowed hard and shook his head. "A graveyard? Wait. That's not good."

Lynn laughed. "Why isn't it?"

"Gives them an easy way to bury us," Adam said.

"You watch too many scary movies," Lynn said.

"Hmm," Marty stared at the map for several moments, deep in

thought. "I don't suppose it'd hurt if we checked the cemetery. We might find some clues."

"Yes!" Dee said, waving a tight fist in the air.

Adam closed his eyes, sighed, and tilted his head back. "Not … another … cemetery."

"What's the worst that can happen?" Dee said.

"Uh, we could all be *killed*," Adam said. His eyes widened for the dramatic effect.

"Not likely during the day," Dee said.

"Death can come at any time," Adam said.

Lynn rolled her eyes. "O—M—G … how about you find a little courage? As I recall, you're fond of saying that you 'laugh in the face of danger.'"

"Take note that I've *not* said that since we went into Tangled Forest. I learned my lesson. I find no reason to tempt fate. But even if I decided to laugh in the face of danger, I'd *never* laugh at the many faces of Death."

Lynn glanced at Dee with a solemn expression. "I vote that we honor him with a shivering chicken badge once this is over."

Dee laughed and shook her head.

Adam frowned. "We don't even have a badge like—"

"We'll make one *special* for you," Lynn said.

"Hey!" Adam said. "I'm not chicken. I'm just … taking precaution. There's nothing wrong with wanting to be safe."

Dee grinned. "We'll be fine as long as we all stick together. What do you think, Marty?"

Marty frowned, studying the map. "We should at least check out the cemetery, but depending upon how large it is, we might not narrow down exactly where the treasure's buried. But there's only one way to know for sure."

"By going?" Lynn asked.

Dee and Marty nodded.

Adam cringed and closed his eyes tightly. "I don't think it's a good idea."

"Then stay here," Dee said. "Watch television."

"Yeah, or suck your thumb," Lynn said with a grin.

Adam shook his head. "Are you kidding? I'm not staying all by myself. What about Ol' Patch? He might still be outside the hotel."

"That's true." Marty nodded. "Come on. Let's look for him from our balcony. Since he was near the back of our hotel, he should be easy to spot, if he's still out there."

Marty slid open the balcony door, eased out to the railing, and peeked down. "I don't see him."

"That's not good," Dee said.

"Why isn't that good?" Lynn asked.

Dee's eyes narrowed with concern. "Because we might stumble into him again since he could've gone any direction."

"There he is," Adam said, pointing. "He's closer to the beach."

They stared in the direction Adam pointed. Ol' Patch was down on one knee, digging in the sand.

"I guess he found something," Marty said.

"That should keep him busy enough. If we hurry, we can go the opposite direction without worrying about him seeing us," Dee said.

CHAPTER 13

The brakes of the city bus screeched as it slowed. The Mystery Solvers were the last tourists on the bus and braced themselves against the back of the seat in front of them during the stop. After the wheels stopped, air released from the brakes making a loud T-S-S! echo.

Marty stood behind Dee, Adam, and Lynn, to allow them to exit the bus before he did.

The black bus driver gave them an odd look as he reached for the handle to open the door. "You guys *sure* you want off here? *Here?*"

Dee nodded. "Yes."

"This is the last time the bus circles the city for the day. So when you need to head back to the beach, call a cab since it's such a long walk. Or, you could visit the cemetery early tomorrow morning when my route starts."

"Thanks, uh—" Marty said, trying to read the man's name on his badge.

"The name's Chuck," he said with a broad grin. His gentle smile was warming as was his rich baritone voice. Slight wrinkles deepened around his lips, his eyes, and across his forehead. His black curled hair was frosted white at the ends.

"Thanks, Chuck, but we can't wait until tomorrow."

"Ah, okay then. But be careful walking around those graves. Some of those old stones have collapsed due to the increasing numbers of sinkholes," Chuck said. His eyes widened as he looked beyond them to the rows of gravestones. "Tales of ghosts in this cemetery are told quite often, if you believe in such things. I've never seen one, but my advice? *Don't* be here after dark."

"We won't," Dee said with a reassuring smile.

"I don't want to be," Adam said softly.

"Okay, good," Chuck said. "Cause I don't want to read about you kids in tomorrow's paper. While I don't think you need to worry about ghosts, bad things have been known to occur here. With that being said, the folks *in* the graves are the lucky ones."

"What do you mean?" Adam asked nervously.

"Ah, it's probably nothing, but the ghosts reportedly seen are those of pirates long dead and gone," Chuck said, putting the bus into park and easing back into his cushioned seat. "Morgan's Cove has a history of pirates who ventured to this cove years ago. Apparently it was a popular hangout for pirates from around the world. Some were known for their ruthless violence. If any pirates are buried in this place, they'd be restless angry spirits now. But, hey, that's my take on it. What brings the four of you out this way anyhow?"

"Curiosity," Marty said with a slight shrug.

Chuck laughed and shook his head. "When I was a kid, my curiosity would have taken me anywhere *except* to a cemetery."

"Mine, too," Adam said softly.

"You're *still* a kid," Lynn said, elbowing his ribs.

"Here, young lady," Chuck said, extending an umbrella in his hand toward her. "You might need this."

Puzzled, she looked at the sky and then back to him. She shrugged her narrow shoulders. "Why? It doesn't look like it's going to rain."

Chuck smiled broadly. "Oh, it'll rain later in the day. Trust me. It rains every day during the summer months. Sometimes only a brief shower and occasionally some severe storms. But that's not why you need the umbrella. You're already starting to get sunburned. Use the umbrella to block the sun. As fair-skinned as you are, you're going to be miserable if you don't get out of the sun soon. So, here."

Lynn shook her head. "I can't take your umbrella."

Chuck smiled warmly. "It's okay. Someone left it on the bus months ago, so I don't think he's going to miss it. Besides, you really need it."

Lynn took the umbrella and offered a slight sheepish smile. "Thanks."

Chuck studied them for several long moments. "So, tell me what's the purpose of those badges you're wearing? You in some sort of club?"

"Dee's Mystery Solvers," Dee said with a broad grin.

"You must be Dee, then, huh?"

She nodded. "How'd you know?"

Lynn rolled her eyes. "How could he *not* know?"

Chuck chuckled. "The pride on your face makes it obvious. It's like a billboard with bright lights, so no mystery there. So you're looking to solve mysteries? What mystery do you expect to uncover in a cemetery? You looking to find the lost treasure of Morgan's Cove?"

Dee shrugged. "I don't know that we will. But we're searching the history of the area right now."

"History, huh? Well … lots of history detailed on those tombstones. It's a shame dead people can't talk or you'd learn far more than what the stones can ever tell you. I imagine they'd tell us differently than what history actually has recorded about them."

Adam, Dee, and Lynn all stared at Marty with sly grins.

Chuck noticed their stares and looked confused. "Am I missing something?"

"No," Marty said, sheepishly grinning and looking away.

Chuck grabbed the lever to pull the door shut. "All right then. I hope you find whatever it is that you're looking for, but keep yourselves out of trouble, okay?"

"You got it," Adam said, crossing his arms and giving a firm nod.

Chuck laughed and pulled the bus door closed. A few seconds later, he drove away.

Dee, Adam, and Lynn stared at Marty after the bus was out of view. "What?" he asked.

Dee sighed. "Have you seen any ghosts yet?"

Marty rolled his eyes. "No."

"You'd keep it a secret now, if you did see one, wouldn't you?" Dee asked.

"Not necessarily," he replied. "But with a cemetery this large, there's always the chance a few ghosts might be moving along the tombstones. They're harder to notice in the daylight though. And as Chuck said, there might be restless violent spirits lingering about, but I'm not going to give you a play-by-play if I do see ghosts."

"What?" Adam asked. "They play football?"

Marty frowned. "You *know* what I mean. I promise to tell you of any ghost or ghosts that are intent on helping or harming us. If they look sinister, I'll shout, 'Run!'"

Adam gulped and his eyes widened.

Lynn snickered.

"I'm not kidding," Marty said. "If I ever yell like that, don't hesitate or ask any questions. Just run."

"You'll really yell like that?"

Marty nodded. "I promise that I'll never do so as a joke, either."

"So nothing yet, huh?" Dee asked.

Marty sighed, turned and faced the gates of the large cemetery, and swept a slow gaze across the downward sloping lawn dotted with aged tombstones. A few people walked along the winding blacktop road that carved its way through the cemetery. Their cars were parked at the edge of the narrow road.

After they walked through the gates, Marty reached into Dee's beach bag and took out the folded map from the pirate shop.

"There's not much to go on," Lynn said.

"You're right," Marty replied. "There isn't."

"Any idea what we should be looking for?" Adam asked.

Marty shook his head. "No. At the time the original map was made, I'd almost bet no graves were here. Well, no *marked* graves."

Dee nodded. "That's probably true."

"So what do we do now?" Adam said, wiping sweat from his face with the hem of his shirt.

"We need to find the oldest spot in this cemetery," Marty replied, folding the map and sticking it into his side pocket. "It could be an unmarked grave and then all the other graves were slowly made around it."

"Seriously?" Adam said, looking around. "There's thousands of graves. That … that'd take days."

"Maybe not," Marty said. "Let's head toward the center. That looks like an old monument or a historical marker underneath the palm tree. Perhaps we can find a clue there."

Lynn stared at the umbrella and then opened it. "I feel silly walking around with this."

"A lot of people use umbrellas to block the sun," Dee said.

Lynn nodded. "At least it's white, so it will reflect the sun effectively."

"That's not necessarily good," Marty said. "If the guy from the pirate shop notices us, the umbrella can be easily spotted."

"You want me to get rid of it?" she asked.

Marty shook his head. "Not unless we see him."

A harsh hot breeze gusted past, almost taking the umbrella out of her hand.

"I guess there's another downside with the wind, too," Adam said.

Lynn held the handle tightly with both hands, fighting the wind's grip, and a few seconds later, the wind ceased. "I never expected that."

"Careful, guys," Marty said softly.

"What is it?" Dee asked. "A ghost?"

Marty nodded.

"Where?" Adam asked.

"Beneath the palm tree."

Dee rose on tiptoes. "The tree we're headed to?"

"Yes."

"Violent or friendly?" Adam asked with wide eyes.

"Trees are neither," Lynn said with a grin.

"The ghost," Adam said.

Marty's eyes focused on the ghost. "From here, there's no way I can tell. Remember if I tell you to run, don't hesitate and don't ask questions. Just do it."

"Brought to you by Nike," Adam said in a deep voice.

Marty frowned at him.

"Sorry," Adam said. "Just trying to lighten the moment."

"I know," Marty said in a low tone. "But this is something all of us need to take seriously, based upon what we know about Morgan Cove's history. Now, you all follow behind me. Let's find out *who* this ghost is."

Marty approached the palm tree with a bit of apprehension. Even though the last ghost he'd seen was friendly and in need of his help, he didn't have any idea what to expect from this one. He never attempted to talk to the ghosts. He'd rather ignore them, so he wasn't certain how he should introduce himself.

Although the map indicated a possible treasure might have been buried somewhere near this spot, he wasn't certain if they were even close. Without knowing the accuracy of the tree's location on the map, he could only estimate that the tree was dead center of the cemetery. Had he been able to view the tree from an airplane overhead, he'd have discovered his guess was correct.

As they came closer, the faint image of the ghost became clearer. He looked to be a boy about their own age, perhaps eleven or twelve years old. His pale blue clothes were baggy, and he wore no shoes.

Marty often wondered why ghosts had clothes, as the spirit was no longer contained by the body, and yet, every ghost he encountered wore a reflection of the attire last worn before death. At least, that was how he rationalized it. Was it because the spirit's memory cast shadows of the attire?

This ghostly boy's face puckered with slight worry and sadness. He longingly gazed at an older couple a few grave rows from the palm tree where he stood. He fretted and wrung his hands together. His lips moved as if he were trying to speak or mumble.

His head turned sharply, perhaps noticing the Mystery Solvers as they approached. The boy's gray eyes swept a gaze across each of them. No hope brightened his sad eyes, until he looked at Marty and made eye contact. His brow rose with sudden excitement.

Marty offered a friendly smile of recognition.

"You can see me?" the boy asked with a slight grin. "You can really see me?"

"Yes. I can," Marty replied.

A smile parted his ghostly lips, followed by a brief squall of laughter. "And your friends? Do they see me as well?"

"No," Marty said. "Only I can see you."

The ghost looked slightly disheartened but still more optimistic than he had been before Marty spoke to him.

"The ghost is talking to you?" Dee asked.

Marty nodded.

"Is it friendly?" Adam asked.

"Tell them, 'Yes!'" the boy said. Eagerness brightened his face. He looked at Dee, Lynn, and Adam and grinned.

Marty grinned. "He is."

"Oh, for hundreds of long painful years I've hoped someone would finally notice me. I'm Herman." He offered his hand momentarily, and then seemed to realize Marty couldn't shake his ghostly hand. "It's indeed a pleasure to speak to you."

"Herman," Marty said with a firm nod, before making quick introductions of the other Mystery Solvers.

"Delighted," Herman said, bowing. "If only they could hear and see me as well. But not a total loss since you do. Although the one with the porcelain skin is of rare beauty."

"She is," Marty agreed.

"What?" Dee asked.

"Nothing." Marty's face reddened. He shook his head and then returned his attention to Herman. "Why are you standing here?"

Herman folded his hands together and rested them at his waist. "Habit, I suppose. Not much else for a ghost to do, especially me. I venture into the city from time to time, but I don't like the progression of change or the way people have changed. They've lost the luster of manners and respect of long ago. And these odd devices they are hypnotized by ... these are the devil's work to be certain."

"You mean these?" Marty slipped his cellphone from his back pocket.

Herman gasped and took a step back. "You're bewitched by them as well?"

"No," Marty said, grinning.

Herman looked confused. "But so many I've seen cannot set them down or look away from them. They're in a trance and some have walked into gravestones or fallen into the street because they weren't watching where they were going."

"Some people get preoccupied with them and don't even realize it. But there are other useful things these phones can do." Marty explained to Herman what all he could do with his phone.

Herman was intrigued. "Maps, really? On that thing? That might have been a lifesaver when I had been alive. Might even have prevented our shipwreck ... who knows?"

"So you were shipwrecked?" Marty asked.

"Yes."

"Was that when you died?"

"Soon after."

"How?"

A sorrowful look claimed Herman's expressions. He looked away. "It's another reason I don't venture into the city."

"Why not?"

"I'm not welcome."

Marty frowned. "Why aren't you welcome in the city? I don't understand."

Herman took a deep breath and released a long slow sigh that revealed the depth of his heartache. "When I washed ashore with the debris from the pirate's ship, and being dressed like this, those in the city refused to help me. I was cold, hungry, and injured. But they ... they would not aid me, not even the priest of their small cathedral. Instead, they beat me with brooms and threw things at me, forcing me to return to the beach where I died from hunger and my injuries. Some of their ghosts linger in the city. Even after death, they condemn and shun me, though they are no better off than I."

"Those ghosts are cursed and unable to travel into the afterlife and they continue to judge you?" Marty asked.

"What's going on?" Dee asked.

Marty held up a finger and waited for Herman to reply.

"Yes," Herman said with a glum face.

Marty took a few seconds to explain to the rest of the club what Herman had told him.

"That's horrible," Lynn said, shaking her head. "Of course, people make false assumptions about me as well."

Herman's brow furrowed and he looked at Marty. "Why would anyone hold any grievance against her?"

"Not so much a grievance, but they judge her for her pale skin and dark makeup," Marty said.

"But ... that's what enhances her beauty."

Marty nodded. "Why would they condemn you after all this time?"

"They blame their deaths on me."

"But you didn't have anything to do with that, did you?" Marty asked.

"Not directly."

"What do you mean?"

Herman looked away with sadness. "When they ran me out of town with the brooms, other pirates witnessed their treatment of me and followed the townsfolk back into town. The pirates protected their own, so they must have killed the townspeople who abused me."

"These ghosts in town who won't welcome you now ... Were they the ones that died back then?"

Herman nodded slowly.

"Ask him about the treasure," Adam said.

Herman gave an odd expression as he glanced toward Adam for a moment and then back to Marty. "What treasure?"

Marty took the map from his pocket and unfolded it. "Legend tells of a treasure being buried near where we are standing."

Herman leaned closer to the map with keen interest and shook his head. "No treasure is hidden here."

"No treasure?" Marty asked. "Are you certain?"

Herman nodded. "Quite. I see that map a lot. Others have come through the graveyard with a similar one. The X is in a different spot on theirs."

"I know," Marty replied. "The X on this map is from the original map we found near those rocks on the shore."

"Those jagged rocks ripped the hull of our ship apart."

"That's where your ship wrecked?" Marty asked.

"Yes, but farther out. The shoreline has changed over the past two centuries."

"Interesting," Marty said.

"What?" Dee and Herman asked at the same time.

"That's where I found the bottle with the original map," Marty said.

Dee shook her head and looked at Lynn and Adam. "This is so frustrating."

Everyone turned toward her, including Herman.

Marty said, "What's frustrating?"

Dee expelled an aggravating sigh. "The two of you are carrying on quite an interesting conversation, but none of the rest of us can even hear the ghost."

"Sorry," Marty and Herman said.

"We need to find a way for all of us to hear these conversations you have, Marty," Dee said.

Re-e-e-ow!

"Pyewackett!" Dee said.

"I wondered if he'd ever pop up," Lynn said, kneeling and scooping the cat into her arms.

Herman's nervous eyes glanced to the black cat. His appearance faded until he was almost invisible.

"Don't go," Marty said.

"I cannot stay within your presence," Herman said.

"Why not?"

"First, you hold the devices that mesmerize all the other people and now, you have a demon cat. Surely the devil is nearby."

"No," Marty said. "He's my cat. I've had him for a couple of years now."

"He wasn't here a few seconds ago. He appeared from nowhere. You cannot tell me—"

"He does have magically abilities, I suppose, but no differently than you," Marty said.

"What?" Herman's eyes widened. "I have no such abilities. Certainly *not* magic!"

"You're disappearing now. I imagine you're able to reappear elsewhere."

"So your cat is a ghost?"

"Yes. At least that's the best way to describe him," Marty replied. "But he's as friendly as a physical cat."

"But she's able to hold him, and the others can see him."

"Yes."

"Then why can't they see me?" Herman asked.

Marty shrugged. "I don't know. A lot of things during your lifetime were based on superstitions and the lack of understanding. Of those things, objects became associated with the devil because their strangeness couldn't be explained. People are afraid of change."

Herman said, "I have seen so many things change over the years and I remain confused by most of these because no one has explained them to me."

"You mentioned that the shoreline has changed," Marty said, pointing at the map. "Then maybe it has affected where the spot should be on the map?"

Herman shook his head and placed his transparent finger to the map. "No. That X covers a small rectangular object, which is barely visible on your map. That was known as the gallows. Many a pirate was hanged in that spot."

"By the townspeople?"

"No, by other pirates. Pirates who believed they had been betrayed by their own."

"Was Peg-leg Jack one of those pirates?" Marty asked.

The mention of the pirate's name caused Herman's eyes to widen. "Indeed. I sailed with him. I watched him hang."

"Legend has it that he was the pirate that buried the treasure," Marty said.

"That's not true," Herman said. "Like me, he survived the shipwreck. But he never buried any treasure. Not here anyway."

Marty frowned. "Are you sure no treasure's buried nearby?"

"Yes. No treasure."

"No treasure?" Adam said.

Marty waved and shushed him. "I'll tell you everything in a few minutes."

"Then why was he hanged?" Marty asked.

"He had angered Captain Morgan about something. The details are quite sketchy," Herman said. "I overhead Peg-leg mention that Morgan would ensure he hanged for his hand in something. What exactly I don't know."

"But there must have been some clue," Marty said. "Do you remember anything else?"

"Come on, Marty," Dee said. "The suspense is killing me."

"One minute," Marty replied.

"We might not have that long," Adam said.

"Why not?"

He pointed. "Jonathan is coming."

"What?" Lynn, Dee, and Marty said at once and turned.

"We need to find a place to hide," Marty whispered. "Now."

"See the big oak tree over there?" Herman asked.

Marty nodded.

"Meet me there." Herman vanished.

"What's he want?" Dee asked.

"Hurry, he wants us to meet him at the large oak."

CHAPTER 15

hen the Mystery Solvers reached the massive oak tree, Marty looked for Herman but didn't see him.

"Is he still here?" Dee asked.

Marty shook his head. "No. At least I don't see him."

"Then what are we going to do?" Adam asked. "Jonathan's heading our direction."

Dee nodded. "Yeah, but he hasn't noticed us."

"That's a good thing," Lynn said, lowering the umbrella enough to hide her and Dee's faces from Jonathan as he came closer.

"He hasn't noticed us *yet*," Adam whispered.

"You should've stayed at the hotel," Lynn said.

Adam frowned but not from anger. He seemed conflicted in coming and possibly wished he *had* stayed at the hotel.

Marty leaned against the huge tree trunk and looked up through the thick branches. He didn't see Herman.

"Psst," Herman whispered. "Around here."

Marty took several steps around the trunk. Herman sat on a lower branch.

Marty said, "He's coming this way. If he sees us, he's going to demand we give him the real map."

"You're afraid of him. Has he threatened you?" Herman looked concerned.

"That's how I felt," Marty replied.

"Climb up here."

"Just me? Or all of us?"

"All of you," Herman replied. "Quickly."

"Why?"

"You'll see."

"Dee," Marty said, "come here."

"What for?"

"Herman wants us to climb up the side of the tree. I'm the tallest, so I can help boost the rest of you up."

"Climb the tree?" Adam asked. "Why? Jonathan will be here soon. He'll see us if we climb up."

"He won't see us behind the tree," Dee said.

She hurried to Marty. He leaned down and cupped his hands together. Dee placed her foot into his hands and allowed him to hoist her upward. She grabbed smaller branches that protruded from the massive branch and pulled herself up and sat down.

"Hurry," Marty said to Lynn. In the same manner, he boosted her up, Dee grabbed her hands and helped her onto the branch beside her. Then Adam hurried up.

"How are you going to get up?" Dee asked.

Marty took a couple of steps back and ran toward the tree, leapt, and grabbed the branch. Dee and Adam each grabbed one of his arms and pulled him onto the wide branch.

"So why are we up here?" Dee whispered.

"Shh!" Adam said, pointing at the narrow road as Jonathan walked past.

Marty glanced at Herman. "Why are we up here?"

"Climb up to the next branch and then look down at the trunk."

"Why?"

"You'll see."

After Jonathan disappeared around the side of a mausoleum, Marty stood and grabbed the next big branch above him. He pulled himself up.

"What are you doing?" Dee asked.

"I'm doing what Herman asked me to do. Give me a second."

Marty used the next layer of smaller branches to keep his balance as he walked to the massive tree trunk. "Wow. I never expected that."

"What?" Lynn and Adam asked.

"This tree is hollow and wide enough for us to climb inside."

"Why would we want to do that?" Adam asked.

Marty shrugged, but they didn't notice his response because of the thick tree foliage.

Herman stood beside Marty. "The roots of this tree have carved tunnels underneath the graveyard. I don't know of any buried treasure, and to my knowledge Peg-leg didn't have any treasure when we washed ashore. He couldn't have carried anything heavy because he'd have sunk in the stormy waters."

"Then why did Captain Morgan have him hanged?"

Herman thought in silence for a while. "I don't remember all that happened. But, if Peg-leg made the map and the mark, he must have hidden something."

"So you think we should climb down into the tree to look around?" Marty asked.

"Why not?"

"The thought of getting trapped underground worries me. Unlike you, we might have a difficult time climbing back out."

"A lot of the tunnels lead back to the surface."

"How do you know that?" Marty asked.

"Surely, you don't think I stand at the palm tree all day."

"I hope not."

"Besides, I've roamed the area over two hundred years …"

"And no treasure?"

"None that I've found, but I've never looked, either."

Marty gave him an odd expression. "Really? You've never tried to find treasure?"

"What's a ghost going to do with gold or silver or jewels?"

Marty chuckled. "Stand guard or protect it."

"Why? It's not mine. I can't spend it. I can't even pick up a single gold piece. Life …" he sighed. "Afterlife is rather boring. Mine is, at least."

Marty shook his head. "I never thought of it like that."

"Until you, no other living human has noticed me. With all the town ghosts hating me, I've had no one to talk to. Loneliness is horrible in life and in death."

"No ghost pirates?" Marty asked.

Fear widened Herman's hollow eyes. "Yes. They're far worse than those ghosts in town. I never venture to where they reside."

"They cannot harm you since you're a ghost," Marty said. "Right?"

"Not physically, since I don't have a body. But psychologically they've tortured other ghosts relentlessly until one either becomes a wrathful spirit like them or forces them to hide in inanimate objects, wreaking havoc on those in the physical realm. I never chose to be a pirate in real life. I've never wanted to cause problems for anyone and certainly not for you and your friends."

"Ma-a-r-ty," Dee whispered with urgency. "Jonathan's circling back."

"Climb down inside the tree," Marty said.

"How will we get out?" Adam asked.

"There are tunnels."

"For real?" Dee asked.

"That's what Herman said," Marty replied.

Marty hurried down the hollow tree, using knots and grooves to place his feet as he climbed down. When he found the last place to secure a handhold, he found nowhere to place his feet. He hung about four feet from the ground. His arms hurt too much from the strain to attempt pulling himself back up. He released the handholds and landed promptly on his feet.

Apparently Dee noticed the slight grooves in the tree bark and used them to lower herself down. When she reached the last handhold, she kicked off her flip-flops. Marty placed his hands under her feet and balanced her, slowly lowering her until she only needed to drop a couple of feet.

$\mathcal{M}$arty watched Lynn lower her foot from the last foothold and he offered his hand to prevent her from loosing her balance. She smiled and took it.

When she was safely on the ground, Marty stepped around her and looked up the hollow tree trunk. Adam placed his ball cap on backwards, gripped a hole inside the trunk, and grunted after lowering himself into the hollow tree. One of his flip-flops dropped, and Marty dodged it. Adam's foot dangled as he attempted to find the next foothold to place his bare toe into.

"A little more to your right," Marty said.

Adam tapped his toe against the wood and slid it until he found the opening. With an awkward descent, he slowly made his way to the bottom and joined the others.

Marty glanced at Herman. "I doubt Jonathan will find us down here."

Herman smiled.

"Maybe not," Dee said, "but why was he in the cemetery in the first place."

"He did seem to be looking for something," Lynn said.

Marty shrugged. "There's no way he knows this is where we went. He wasn't on the bus."

"Which means he was probably already here," Dee said.

"Could've been," Marty replied.

Adam wiped his hands on his shorts and his nervous eyes glanced around the dim tunnel.

"Follow me," Herman said.

Marty looked at the others. "Come on."

The long tunnel was made by a huge root that had rotted away over the past century, making Marty wonder how the tree was still partly alive.

Dee tapped Marty's shoulder. "Did Herman tell you where he's leading us?"

Marty shook his head.

"Tell her," Herman said, "I'm going to show you a different way out of the cemetery."

Marty told them.

"Re-e-ow!"

Herman vanished.

Adam and Lynn squealed.

Marty sighed. "Pyewackett. You need to warn us when you're going to appear."

Dee released her held breath. "I agree."

"Herman?" Marty said. "Where are you?"

"He left?" Adam said in a nervous whisper.

"I think so," Marty said. "At least, he's invisible. Herman? It's just our cat."

Marty peered ahead in the dim tunnel, but couldn't see the slightest image of Herman. "Come on. We need to find a way out."

Lynn used her flashlight app to brighten the narrow tunnel.

"Did Herman come back?" Adam asked.

"No. But, he said earlier that several tunnels lead to the surface. Let's follow this one for a ways."

"And if it's a dead end?" Lynn asked.

Adam swallowed hard. "We go back to the tree."

Dee snickered.

"What's funny?" Adam asked.

"None of us can reach the lowest groove to pull ourselves up," Dee replied.

"We could stand on Marty's shoulders," Adam said.

"You can't climb the rope in gym class," Marty said. "You certainly can't climb up the tree with all the hidden handholds you'd have to find."

"Besides," Lynn said. "How would *he* get back up?"

"Let's just follow the tunnel," Marty said. "Dee, you should reconsider the name of our club."

"Only for one individual," Dee said. "It's hard to solve mysteries when Adam's afraid of his own shadow."

"I am not."

"Arguing isn't making any progress," Marty said. "Herman's more skittish than Adam, though."

"See?" Adam said.

"That's not necessarily a compliment," Lynn said.

Dee shook her head. "I'd never expect a ghost to be so timid."

Pyewackett mewed softly and ran ahead of them.

"That is odd," Lynn said. "Why would a ghost be scared of anything?"

Marty said, "Perhaps, it's due to him suffering traumatic circumstances and dying at such a young age."

"That's part of it," Herman said, appearing as a floating image ahead of them.

The four Mystery Solvers froze in their tracks and released short screams.

Herman's eyes widened. "All of you can see me?"

"I can," Dee said.

"Me, too," Lynn replied.

Adam nodded.

"How?" Herman asked.

Pyewackett mewed again.

"I think Pyewackett is the reason," Marty said.

"Your cat?" Herman asked.

"Yes."

Herman placed his ghostly feet on the tunnel floor and his image stabilized. "Maybe I shouldn't be so afraid of him."

"You shouldn't be at all," Dee said. "He's a cat."

"He's a black cat," Herman said.

"A cat's a cat," Adam said with a frown.

"Not during the time when I was alive. A black cat was associated with witches and the Devil," Herman said.

"Pyewackett's not," Dee said. "He's a sweet cat with a bit of … okay, he has some abilities that could be considered magical, but he's never caused harm to anyone or anything. Without his help, only Marty could see you. Is that bad luck?"

Herman stared at the cat for a few moments and then he shook his head. He grinned. "No. That's the best luck I've had in a couple hundred years."

"Shh!" Marty said. "Listen."

Everyone hushed and their eyes widened. Lynn pressed the flashlight beam from her cellphone against her chest to hide the light.

Two deep voices echoed farther down the tunnel. The men were apparently talking to one another but their words weren't understandable from the distance.

Marty looked at Herman. "Are people usually down here?"

"Sometimes."

"For what purpose?" Dee asked.

Herman shrugged. "I don't know. I tend to keep my distance from voices I don't recognize."

"Are they ghosts?" Adam asked.

Herman chuckled. "Even I can't tell just by hearing them."

"I've never heard ghosts talking," Adam said. "Well, except for you."

"How do you know?" Herman asked. "Have you ever heard voices but never found out who was talking?"

Adam thought for a moment. "Maybe. It's hard to say."

"Even if you can't see ghosts," Herman said, "there are times when you'll hear them without knowing it's ghosts."

"Let's keep quiet," Marty said. "We'll sneak closer to see what's going on and if we can find a way out without them seeing us."

Dee nodded. "Sounds good to me."

CHAPTER 17

The tunnel widened into a cross-section. Straight ahead, several lightbulbs glowed above a couple of foldout tables. Two men sat at the table with various pieces of jewelry. One man was looking at the stone through a loupe. The rings' gems flickered in the light. Marty was certain these two individuals weren't ghosts.

Marty motioned Dee and the others to stand against the wall of the intersecting tunnel, so the two men wouldn't see them. He stood against the wall on the opposite side of the intersection.

"What are they doing?" Dee whispered.

Marty shrugged. "I'm not sure."

Herman stepped to the center of the tunnel. "I can find out."

"What if they see you?" Dee asked.

Herman made a soured expression. "That's doubtful. You four have been the only living people who've ever acknowledged me."

"But what if that's changed now?" Adam whispered.

Herman smiled. "Then I can finally scare someone else for a change."

Herman walked toward the tables where the two men sat. The men were too preoccupied studying the rings and necklaces to have noticed the ghost, if they could see him.

Marty grinned, watching Herman step between the men's chairs.

Herman peered at the objects on the table and placed his ghostly hand on one ring, apparently trying to move it, but he wasn't able to. Neither man noticed his hand. Discouraged, Herman made his way back to Marty and the others.

"Well?" Dee asked with raised brows.

"Lots of rings, bracelets, and necklaces," Herman replied.

Dee glanced at Marty. "You think they've found the treasure?"

"Maybe?" he replied.

Adam whined. "Aww."

"I've never heard of any buried treasures though," Herman said.

"What have ya found?" a familiar deep voice bellowed near the tables. The two men jerked their heads and fastened their attention on Jonathan, who stood a few inches from the table.

"Sheesh, John," one man said. "You trying to give me a heart attack?"

"No, Trent," Jonathan replied. "I want to know if you've found the treasure yet?"

Trent shook his head, took a deep breath, and released it slowly. "George and I haven't found anything in the old graves except jewelry. Mind you, some of these could bring you a small fortune. People love vintage rings and jewelry."

"What makes you still believe in the treasure that's nothing more than a legend?" George asked.

"George," Jonathan said, "because some children found the real map today."

"How do you know that?" George asked.

"They were carrying the bottle that it was stored inside. The cork residue was fresh around the bottle's top, so they took something out of the bottle."

"So?" Trent said. "That doesn't mean the real map was in the bottle."

"You didn't see the expression on the kid's face when I asked about the bottle's contents. Kids aren't good at lying. I could tell by his eyes and his nervousness that he was lying. They have the map."

George shook his head. "You've a way of scaring most adults with your hardened attitude, John. I imagine you did quite the job of scaring this kid. It's more likely he was afraid of you than he was lying."

"Nonsense!" Jonathan said. "He has the map!"

"Jonathan, you've obsessed over the Peg-leg's treasure since you were a kid. Maybe it's time you accepted it as nothing more than a legend."

Jonathan's eyes narrowed. "Every legend holds some truth. No one's ever found Peg-leg's treasure. It's still here."

"John," George said. "You need to accept that either the treasure wasn't real or someone found it long ago and never told anyone else."

"Peg-leg was hanged and refused to tell where he'd hidden the treasure, even to spare his own life," Jonathan said. "The truth died with him."

"Okay," Trent said. "Let's say you're right. The treasure exists. What do you want us to do? On these tables alone, you've at least a hundred thousand dollars worth of jewelry. Along with all the previous boxes of jewelry we've taken from the coffins, we're setting on a pretty penny. Let the fantasy go."

"It's not a fantasy," Jonathan said. "The actual treasure still exists, which is worth far more than all the measly trinkets we've gotten."

"Okay, fine," Trent said. "What do you want us to do? We're kinda busy grading the jewels."

"Work faster."

Trent leveled a harsh glare at Jonathan.

"Meaning?" George asked.

"Keep pillaging the oldest graves. The tunnels expose the oldest coffins, so we don't have to dig them up. You just have to break through the rotten planks to get what's inside."

"You think the treasure's buried in a grave?" Trent asked.

"Where else could it be?"

"Okay, we'll keep looking," Trent said.

Jonathan's jaw tightened. "Comb through at least another twenty graves before the sun sets."

George shook his head. "We'll try. That's a lot of graves."

"Do what you can then. You'll get your cut as soon as we sell the jewelry. Watch your phones, too. I'll text you whenever I find those kids. We'll find a way to make them talk."

Jonathan stormed away, taking another path in the opposite direction of the intersection where Dee and the Mystery Solvers stood.

Dee, Marty, Adam, and Lynn all exchanged nervous glances. Their danger wasn't from a ghost. Their greatest danger was Jonathan, even more than what Marty had feared during their first encounter with the man.

CHAPTER 18

Marty swallowed the hard lump in his throat, watching the two seated men after Jonathan disappeared down a different corridor. "They're grave robbers."

Dee's brow rose. "This is horrible. We need to contact the police."

Adam lowered to a crouch. "We best do something before they see us."

"How do we get out of here?" Marty whispered to Herman. "At the moment, our only choices are to the right or left of the intersecting paths. We need to get to the surface before Jonathan finds us."

Herman looked confused. "Let's go to the right. Or maybe, it's the left? No, the right."

"You don't know?" Dee asked.

"To be honest, since I'm a ghost, I've never had to follow any of them out." Herman stared at the path to the right of the intersection. "I can go through walls and the dirt."

Dee rolled her eyes. "Great."

"Shh!" Marty placed a finger to his lips.

The two men's voices became louder.

"Looks like John's paranoia is out of hand, again," Trent said.

"You think?" George replied. "He wants us to help him catch kids because he thinks they have the real map."

"Not happening," Trent said.

"You're going to tell him, 'no'?"

"You bet, if he plans to go after kids."

"You won't get your share," Trent said.

George laughed. "I don't care. You can't spend money in prison."

"That's true."

"Besides, we've found thousands of dollars of jewelry in this cemetery," George said. "He should be satisfied with that."

Trent shook his head. "Greed's hunger never lessens, which is why he obsesses over a treasure that probably doesn't exist."

A loud thwack echoed down the tunnel behind Marty and the other Mystery Solvers.

George and Trent stood and exchanged glances.

"What was that?" Trent asked.

George frowned and stepped around the table. "Let's go find out."

CHAPTER 19

*M*arty jumped and turned in the direction of the noise. Chills shot down his spine. "What was that?"

"I'm sorry," Lynn said. "I think it was my umbrella. I left it at the top of the tree. It must've fallen."

Dee's eyes widened. "Uh, Marty, we need to find a place to hide. They're coming."

"I realize that. But if I come into the intersection, they'll see me for sure. You guys run that way, and I'll go this way."

"No-o-o," Dee said. "We stick together."

"It's safer this way," Marty said.

"No," Dee said. "I'm the leader of the Mystery Solvers and I say that you come with us. You're the strongest and fastest of us, so we need you to protect us."

"They'll see me."

Dee shrugged. "They're going to see all of us if we don't hurry. Now, come on, please."

Marty wanted to protest further, but she was right. They didn't have time to argue. And if the passageway to the right was a dead end, they were all in trouble anyway. They'd be caught. However, if the path led to the surface, they could attract the attention of anyone else in the cemetery by yelling for help.

"Who's there?" George asked, cautiously heading into the dim tunnel.

"Now, Marty!" Dee shouted.

Marty sprinted across the intersection, past Dee and the others, and hurried into the narrowing tunnel.

"Hey! Come back here!" Trent shouted.

The sounds of bare feet pounding the hard dirt floor thudded behind Marty. A high pitched squeal rose behind him. At first he thought it was Lynn or Dee, but glancing over his shoulder, he discovered it was Adam. Panic claimed Adam's facial features. He was so frightened that he probably didn't realize he was screaming.

The incident would've been funny if they weren't fearful of getting hurt or losing their lives. Although Trent and George didn't act like they wanted to help Jonathan, there was no guarantee that they'd allow the Mystery Solvers to escape. At the least, the two men would capture them and hold them until Jonathan arrived.

Herman's luminous form appeared ahead of Marty in the tunnel where the path split. He pointed to the right. "Go that way."

Marty wondered if he should trust Herman's directions since the ghost seemed not to know where the tunnels led. There was little choice though.

Marty reached back and grabbed someone's hand. He wasn't certain who was running behind him, but he felt better knowing someone was close. "Herman says to go right!"

The tunnel narrowed, causing Marty to slow his speed. Several rocks were blocking the path. They could no longer run.

"Come on," Marty whispered.

A bright light burst into his eyes. He squinted and raised a hand to shield his eyes.

When the light turned to the floor and the spots faded, Lynn was smiling at him, holding his hand. "I figure we could use some light now."

Marty grinned. "Good idea. They already know we're here. Light can help us escape quicker."

She squeezed his hand slightly.

Dee stumbled into Lynn's back. "What's the hold up? Keep moving."

"Yeah!" Adam said, panting. "I hear them coming."

"Be careful," Marty said. "There's a pile of rocks."

Marty stepped over the rocks, still holding Lynn's hand and helping her across. Dee and Adam were quick to scramble over the rocks and follow.

Lynn shone her light in the direction they had come for a few seconds, but the two men weren't visible yet. The men's heavy panting was getting closer and occasionally, their groaning complaints could be heard. The only advantage the Mystery Solvers had over their pursuers was the men couldn't move through the narrow tunnel as fast as they could.

Marty held the hope that they might escape before those men caught up to them.

"Jonathan," one of the men said loudly while panting. "Those kids you were talking about ... they're in the tunnel. Yep. Heading toward the shoreline exit."

Marty clutched Lynn's hand tighter. His stomach tightened. He guessed the man was talking to Jonathan on his cellphone. Marty clutched Lynn's hand and hurried through the dark tunnel. He knew they didn't have much time to escape, if they had any time left at all.

CHAPTER 20

arty stared in near disbelief. Herman's ghost lofted near what appeared to be a dead end in the tunnel. He feared their hope to escape was over. But once they reached Herman, the tunnel curved slightly to the right and the crashing ocean waves on the beach echoed nearby.

A curtain of ivy hung behind where Herman stood. Light beamed through small cracks, which seemed odd for various reasons. For one, thick ivy didn't grow so close to salt water or in pure sand. The leaves were too waxy to be real, too. They felt like plastic.

"What are we going to do?" Lynn asked.

Marty glanced down the tunnel. Dee and Adam weren't far behind, but were still getting over the rocks.

"We need to get out of here," he said.

Marty shoved his shoulder to pass through the ivy strands, but instead, the old planks covered with ivy dropped onto the wet sand. The evening sunlight spilled into the narrow crevice.

Marty squeezed Lynn's hand and pulled. He glanced over his shoulder at Dee and Adam. "Come on, hurry!"

The wet beach where they exited was enclosed by rocky ledges that formed a U-shape. This section of the beach was separated from most tourists. The ledges weren't high enough to be considered cliffs, but since he and the other Mystery Solvers were barefoot, climbing the rocks would be precarious, at best. The sharp rocks would cut their feet like broken glass.

A quick survey revealed no curious tourists combing the shore for shells. No lifeguards. A posted sign warned to swim at your own risk. With the swell of the tide coming in, they couldn't safely swim out and around the rocks. The only route they had was to find a way to cross the ledge.

Marty and Lynn took several steps away from the opening. He hoped to find a smooth path up the ledge that others had used, but—

"Where do you think you're going?" Jonathan asked, jumping off the small sand dune and landing in front of Marty. "I want my map. *Now.*"

"I'm afraid I can't help you with that," Marty said.

"The map isn't yours." Lynn's fingers tightened around Marty's.

"Marty!" Dee yelled.

Adam screamed. "Let her go!"

Marty turned to see one of the men grab Dee's arm and pull her back into the mouth of the tunnel. Anger heated Marty's face. He took a step toward the tunnel. "Hey! Let my sister go!"

Jonathan placed a firm hand around Marty's throat and squeezed slightly. The man's dark menacing eyes sent a chill through Marty. "I want the map. No need to keep lying about not having it. Give it to me, and your sister and the others can leave. Got it?"

Marty opened his mouth to protest, but Dee held up her phone. "The police are on their way."

The man holding her arm jerked the phone from her free hand. He glanced at the screen, tucked her phone into his back pocket, and shook his head. "She's not called anyone."

Dee gritted her teeth and growled with anger, trying to pull free without any success.

"Trent," Jonathan said, "get their phones."

Trent nodded.

Jonathan sneered, placing his hand on his knife. "It doesn't matter. Even if you contacted the police, they'd never find you in those tunnels."

He glared at Marty. "I want the map, and you're going to give it to me. Understood?"

Marty read the threat in Jonathan's evil glare. While at the pirate shop, he had entertained the thought about Jonathan possibly playacting as a sinister pirate, but now, the man's lack of reason wasn't questionable. The man's intent was vicious and violent. He feared what Jonathan was capable of doing. Even if Marty attempted to fight the man, he wasn't strong enough to beat him, especially with Jonathan's hand on the knife.

Marty nodded. "Okay, fine. The map's yours. I'll give it to you, but I don't have it on me. It's at our hotel."

"Don't give him the map," Dee said.

Jonathan grinned. "See? I knew you were lying."

"Let us go and I'll give you the map," Marty said.

"Marty, don't," Dee said.

"I don't have any other choice, Dee," Marty said. "No mystery's worth our lives."

"Now, you're talking some sense," Jonathan said.

"Let us go," Marty said, "and I'll give you the map."

"No, that's not how it's going to work," Jonathan said. "Trent, you drive our new friend to his hotel and make sure he gets you the map. George and I will stay here with the others. You've got an hour to return with the map. Otherwise, things are going to get bad for your friends."

Trent hurried to Marty and Jonathan grabbed Lynn's wrist and tugged her away from Marty.

Marty formed fists and turned toward Jonathan. "Let her go."

Jonathan laughed. "Boy, you're no match for us. Do what I told you to do and you'll all be let go. Don't try to be a hero and do something stupid and something you'll regret."

Adam was near tears, but it didn't seem that he was scared. His frustration of helplessness overshadowed him.

Jonathan pulled the knife from its sheath and waved George to go inside the tunnel. "All of you, inside, now!"

Jonathan followed them into the tunnel.

After they were out of sight, Marty glanced at Trent.

Trent sighed. He didn't seem too eager to follow Jonathan's demands. He motioned Marty by tilting his head. "Come on."

Trent wore nice cargo shorts, expensive running shoes, and placed chrome-rimmed glasses to cover his eyes. He didn't seem to desire the pirate wannabe attitude Jonathan childishly displayed.

"You don't have to do this," Marty said.

Trent walked to the rocks and started up. "I don't *want* to do this, kid, but yes, I *have* to."

"You're afraid of him?" Marty cautiously placed his foot onto the rocks.

"You best be, too," Trent replied.

"Why?"

"None of his threats are ever made lightly."

"Meaning?"

"Meaning … if I don't return with you and that map … let's not even think of what he might do."

"He's capable of murder?"

Trent didn't reply. He paused in step for a moment and then continued walking.

"Has he ever killed someone?" Marty pressed.

"Look, the less you know, the better, especially if you want him to let you and your friends go when we return."

"So he has?"

"Keep going, kid," Trent said. "A half hour passes pretty fast."

"We took the bus out here," Marty said. "There's no way we can—"

"My car is nearby. Come on."

CHAPTER 21

*D*ee sat at the table with Adam and Lynn. They stared at the jewelry. The multicolored gems flickered under the hanging light bulbs. She'd never seen such beauty and had never held much desire for owning a lot of fancy jewelry, but she recognized the lure such stunning gems beckoned. For a moment, she couldn't pry her gaze from them.

"You're never going to get away with this." Dee frowned, flicking her attention at Jonathan. She crossed her arms.

Jonathan's eyes narrowed. "Ask the last people who discovered what I was doing."

Dee, Lynn, and Adam exchanged puzzled and nervous glances. Dee swallowed hard and wished Marty was with them. She worried that Trent might hurt her brother and she'd never see him again. An hour of waiting would seem an eternity. She whispered a prayer and regretted not hitting 9-1-1 on her phone before it was snatched from her hand.

"Ah, well, sorry. Ya can't." Jonathan sneered. A moment later, he laughed. "They're no longer able to talk."

Dee frowned. "You killed them?"

George cleared his throat and shook his head. In a near whisper, he said, "It's best you keep your questions to yourselves."

"So you're grave robbers?" Dee asked.

"You can't steal from the dead," Jonathan said. "They've no use of gold and jewels, now do they?"

"It doesn't give you the right to take it," Dee said.

"No one knows, so no one will care."

Dee looked at an old coffin with its side ripped open. Bones and cloth was all she could see. "Ghosts exist. Sometimes, they come back to claim what was theirs."

Jonathan laughed. "Do you believe such nonsense?"

George's eyes filled with fright.

"He does," Dee said, pointing at George. "Don't you?"

George remained silent.

"I'm surprised you and your partner worked so long around these dead bodies," Dee said. "Knowing that you're stealing from them, shouldn't you fear vengeance?"

Jonathan reared back his head and laughed harder. He bellowed deeply and when he finally stopped, he wiped tear from his eye. He walked to one of the busted open caskets that rested on a hard earthen surface. "Ya see what remains, young lass?" He returned to using his pirate voice as he had in the pirate shop. "Much less occupies a grave after the flesh has decomposed, which means, there's room for me to shove more into the grave—like your bodies!"

Adam whispered, "Dee, please, for once, don't keep talking."

Dee paled and even without Adam's stern plea, she found herself at a loss for words. Her imagination placed her into the scenerio with Jonathan actually putting their dead bodies into the underground coffins. Tears filled her eyes.

Since no one else knew about these tunnels under the cemetery, Dee and Marty's mother and their families probably would never find their remains if Jonathan carried out his threat. Most people searching for them would believe they'd drown and been pulled out into the ocean.

She hoped Jonathan was bluffing as a means to simply silence her and get the map he coveted. But, she couldn't be sure. Things as bad as what she pictured were on the news and in the papers from time to time. Crazy, evil people existed. Tourists disappeared all around the world, never to be seen again. And Jonathan's sinister nature with his volatile threats were a prelude to what might happen next.

Her hint about ghosts was a cue to summon Herman into action, but she could no longer see him. Had he gone with Marty? Where was Pyewackett? If Herman remained behind with them, were they unable to see the ghost because Marty wasn't there?

Dee uncrossed her arms and set her hands on the table. The smartest thing she could do was to not say anything further. No sense stirring up the anger of a demented individual by being mouthy.

Jonathan walked to the narrow tunnel. "George, keep an eye on them. I'll be back soon."

CHAPTER 22

Marty rode in the passenger seat of Trent's olive green Jeep. After several failed attempts to start a conversation with Trent, Marty was about to give up.

Trent sat in silence, chewing his lower lip, and he seemed to be brooding. It was obvious Jonathan was forcing Trent to do something he didn't want to do. Marty figured that if he could somehow break the ice, he might persuade Trent to help them.

Trent's Jeep wasn't new, but it wasn't a clunker, either. He kept the interior almost pristine. To live near a beach, few grains of sand were on the floor mats. The dash console and the divider between the bucket seats were polished. He invested time in keeping his vehicle maintained. Perhaps his association with Jonathan was for financial gain to get something better, but Trent didn't harbor the greedy glint in his eyes and was content with what he had.

Trent parked the Jeep at the curb across the street from the hotel. He faced Marty. "Look, let's hurry and get the map for Jonathan. Just cooperate and it'll be easier to convince him to let you all go."

Convince? The word caused Marty instant uneasiness.

Marty frowned. "You don't think he'll release us?"

"Just cooperate. George and I will ensure that you're released."

"Has Jonathan ever killed anyone?"

Trent appeared conflicted in answering, as if doing so was betrayal. "No. He's not killed anyone, but he's hurt some people lately. He's probably capable of much worse when provoked."

"Provoked? We've done nothing to provoke him. *We* found the map, which makes it rightfully ours. For us to keep it, isn't provoking him."

Trent nodded. "I understand. Believe me, I agree. But Jonathan's never harmed children before but seeing his actions, he's sunken to a new low. I don't want to see you or your friends hurt, but you saw the look his eyes. His obsession has gotten out of hand. I don't know how far he'd go, and I really don't want to find out, okay?"

Marty nodded. "Then why keep hanging around him in the first place? Call the police."

Trent shook his head. "No. That's the last thing you want to do. We'd all be in worse danger if you did that. He might snap."

"What's to say that he hasn't already?" Marty asked. "His actions indicate he's beyond reasonable. He's a thief and you're an accessory."

Trent flinched before opening his door. "Come on. We're wasting precious time. Let's just do this so you and your friends can return to your normal lives."

Marty opened his door and stepped onto the sidewalk. Trent was somewhat friendly, despite the situation, and that troubled Marty. It was almost the 'good cop/bad cop' performance with Jonathan far worse than bad. Marty wanted to believe that Trent was being upfront and honest and truly wanted to help them escape, but deep down, Marty remained wary.

Crossing the street, Marty glanced toward the boardwalk. Ol' Patch was packing his gear and noticed Marty. Marty paused in step, but Trent eased beside him and gripped his arm, tugging Marty to keep going. Ol' Patch made a curious frown and stiffened with concern. Marty made a pleading expression to Ol' Patch, indicating he was in trouble.

CHAPTER 23

*I*n the motel room, Marty retrieved the map from beneath the bed. He handed it to Trent. "There. Can we get back to the cemetery? I've kept my part of the bargain."

Trent shrugged. "That was quicker than I expected."

"What did you expect me to do? I don't have time to haggle and the map's certainly not worth losing my friends over."

After descending the elevator and hurrying through the lobby, Marty and Trent made their way across the street to the Jeep. Ol' Patch propped himself against the fender of the passenger side and offered a tired smile.

"Patch?" Trent said. "What are you doing?"

"Ah, getting ready to head home. Mind giving me a lift?"

"Sorry, I don't have time. Please, get off my Jeep." Trent pressed the button on his key ring to unlock the door.

Marty glanced at Ol' Patch and then to Trent with confusion. "You two know one another?"

"Everyone in the Cove knows Patch," Trent replied.

Trent never saw Patch's arm move. Marty only happened to see the blur of Ol' Patch's fist as it smashed the side of Trent's jaw. Trent collapsed on the pavement.

Marty was stunned but grinned, thinking how Ol' Patch only had one eye and Trent had both but Trent had been blind to the punch.

Ol' Patch glanced around. "We'd best get a moving."

Ol' Patch grabbed the keys and Marty picked up the rolled map. Ol' Patch hurried and dragged Trent around to the sidewalk. Patted down Trent's pockets and took his cellphone. He placed his metal detector and backpack in the rear of the Jeep.

"Hop in," Ol' Patch said. "Where are your friends?"

"At the cemetery."

"What's going on?" Patch looked at the rolled parchment in Marty's hand. "That was in the bottle?"

Marty nodded.

"A map?"

"Yeah. We think it is the authentic map. Jonathan's holding my sister and friends at an underground tunnel in the cemetery and has given me an hour to return with the map."

"Well, let's take it to him." Patch grinned.

Marty studied Patch for a few moments and then frowned. "Wasn't your patch on the other eye earlier?"

Patch's grin faded. He peeled the patch off his eye and laughed. He winked. "What do you know? Must be a miracle, eh?"

"You're not missing an eye?"

"No."

"Then why the charade?"

Patch turned right at the intersection and sped up. He shrugged. "People tend to leave me alone. For some reason, they view me as a creepy ol' vagrant, which suits me fine. Gives me more privacy while I comb the beach."

"I see."

"Ha! Good one," Patch said. "You and your friends thought I was creepy. Don't lie. Facial expressions are easy to read. I could tell you wanted to get far away from me when I first spoke to you."

"Sorry."

"Oh, don't be. Kids should always take precautions with strangers."

"How do you know Trent?"

Patch grinned. "Went to school with him a long time ago. So what got you on Jonathan's bad side? I tried to steer you away from that shop. Did he see the bottle you showed me?"

Marty nodded. "Yes. He immediately lost his mind and threatened me."

"How'd you and your friends end up in the cemetery with him?"

Marty explained their bus ride to the cemetery, the hollow tree, and the tunnels. "Jonathan and his friends are grave robbers."

"They're taking stuff from the graves?"

"Yes. Gold and jewelry. Trent and ... I think the other guy is George?"

Patch nodded. "Those two get messed up in all sorts of trouble."

"They were sorting jewelry on a table under the cemetery."

"Doesn't surprise me. They've broken in my house a few times."

"Really?"

Patch nodded. "Yep."

"What did they steal?"

"Nothing that I noticed."

"Then how do you know they broke in?" Marty asked.

Patch laughed. "I've got surveillance cameras and watched them go through my stuff."

"You didn't call the police?"

"Not yet. If they'd taken something, I would, and if they ever do, I have it all on video. But, looks like they're going to jail now, anyway. Holding your friends hostage to steal your map will lock them away for some time, especially with you being minors."

"What do you think they were looking for in your house?" Marty asked.

"That map you found."

"Really?"

Patch nodded. "He's wanted to find that treasure for as long as I have and perhaps *more* than I do. I'd never do what he's done, threatening kids. Since I'm always searching the beaches and the area for clues of where that treasure was buried, he probably suspects I found the map or that I already found the treasure."

Patch kept the speed of the Jeep right at the limit. The late afternoon breezed flowed pleasantly through the open windows.

"Do you know what the treasure is?"

Patch shook his head. "No, but that's the fun of it, isn't it? The mystery. That's the best part of the hunt."

"Yeah. That's what my sister and two friends do. She formed the Mystery Solvers club and when we found the map, it was our next mystery to solve."

Patch grinned. "Sounds like you have a lot of fun. But let me ask you a question."

"Sure."

"If you found the map, why did you go to Jonathan's shop?"

"To buy their map."

Patch frowned. "Why?"

"Well, placing the new map over the old one helped us find current landmarks and better align where the X on the map is."

"Ah, smart. Once we get your friends away from Jonathan, do you mind if I helped you find the treasure? I don't want a cut from it or anything. I'd like to satisfy my old curiosity."

Marty grinned and nodded. "Sure. We could use your help. But, I've been told that there's no treasure left behind by Peg-leg Jack."

"No? Who told you that?"

"Re-e-ow!"

Patch jolted up in his seat and veered the Jeep side to side on the highway. "What the—? How'd that cat get up here? Trent has a cat?"

Marty patted the passenger seat and shook his head. "The cat's mine. Come on, Pyewackett."

"Yours?"

"Yep."

"You brought him?"

"No. It's a long story."

Patch placed a hand over his heart and sighed. "One I hope you'll share later. 'bout scared me into an accident."

"Yeah, he does that."

CHAPTER 24

fter they got out of the Jeep near the hollow tree, Marty sprinted to its other side. He climbed up through the branches.

Patch stared up through the branches. "Why are we climbing a tree? The graves are in the ground."

"You'll see. Come on," Marty said.

Patch chuckled and shook his head. "I'm not as spry as I once was."

Patch made an awkward climb through the branches, careful where he placed his hands and feet. Marty waited at the top with his patience lessening by the second.

"The inside of the tree is hollow, so we have to climb down. There's a slight drop near the bottom but not far enough to hurt you," Marty said.

Patch stared in disbelief. "Never would I have expected this."

Marty grinned. "I know."

"Re-ow!"

"Sheesh!" Patch almost fell backwards but grabbed a tree branch and held fast. "Didn't we leave that cat in the Jeep? How'd he get up here so quickly?"

"He's prone to appear and disappear at any time."

Herman appeared on the other side of the broken treetop.

"What are you doing?" Marty asked. "Why aren't you with Dee and the others?"

Patch frowned. "What are you talking about?"

"Sorry," Marty said. "I'm talking … hmm … something else I should explain and you're going to think it's weird. But I'm not crazy."

Patch grinned. "That's usually the first line an unstable person says."

Marty explained the cat and then about Marty's ability to see ghosts ever since he got the cat.

"Okay, whatever you say," Patch said. "Not judging you. And I'm not saying that I buy into this. I'm here to help you get your sister and friends back. So, let's go."

Herman shook his head. "Marty, you need to be careful. Jonathan's not Jonathan."

Marty frowned. "What do you mean?"

"I—," Patch said.

"Not you," Marty whispered.

"Ah, the … ghost, eh?" Patch rolled his eyes.

Marty nodded.

Herman said, "Captain Morgan's ghost has control over Jonathan's mind and body. That's why I'm up here. If he sees me, he'll try to cause me great harm. He's far more powerful than I remember."

"How?"

"Since he possesses a physical body, he's grown stronger."

"But how can he hurt you? You're a spirit," Marty said.

Marty turned to Patch. "Have you ever known Jonathan to be violent?"

Patch frowned. "No. He's a drunk and thief, but he's never acted violently. Why?"

"That's not the first impression he gave me," Marty said softly. "I know you're having a difficult time believing there's a ghost talking to me, but Herman—"

"Herman?"

"Yes. He said that Captain Morgan's ghost possesses Jonathan, so he's stronger than normal."

Patch stared at Marty in disbelief.

"Look," Marty said, "I understand if you think I'm crazy. That's why I never tell others about my … ability. I only recently told Dee and—"

Patch shook his head and pointed. "No. Is that Herman? Wearing blue pants and—"

Herman's eyes widened. "He can see me!"

Pyewackett mewed.

Marty scratched behind the cat's ears and whispered, "Thanks."

"How do you know Captain Morgan's ghost is inside Jonathan?" Patch asked.

"I recognize his angered spirit. It's been a while since he's come to the cemetery."

Patch scratched his chin. "Is there any way to draw Captain Morgan out of Jonathan?"

Herman frowned, thinking, before giving a sly grin. "I'm not sure. There might be a way."

"If you think of a way, tell me," Patch said.

"We need to give the map to Jonathan," Marty said, climbing down.

"Not yet," Herman said.

"Why not?"

Herman looked uneasy. "Because he's liable to attack you."

Patch chuckled. "He's going to attack us anyway."

"Why do you say that?" Marty asked.

"He's not going to like that I'm here and Trent's not. Tuck that map into one of these holes in the hollow tree trunk," Patch said. "We can retrieve it later."

"He's certain to attack us then," Marty said.

"Maybe," Patch said. "But he'd be less likely to kill us. He wants that map. Jonathan's always been obsessed to find the treasure, but he's the kind of person who'd rather secretly steal it. He's never physically hurt or held people against their will. That might be why Captain Morgan possessed him. He recognizes Jonathan's greed."

Marty realized the danger of provoking an angry ghost. "Do you think you can defeat a man possessed by a madman's ghost?"

Patch shrugged. "I guess we're going to find out."

CHAPTER 25

After Marty, Herman, and Patch reached the tunnel, Marty started to lead the way to where the jewelry was being sorted by Trent and George. Patch grabbed his arm and shook his head.

"What?" Marty asked.

"I can't let you go in first. Just tell me which way to go."

"Straight ahead. When you reach the intersection, keep going straight."

Patch nodded.

Herman lofted above the ground and drifted past Patch, stopping just short of walking into the room where Dee and the others were. He gave Patch a fearful glance and shook, nearly going invisible.

"Jonathan!" Patch shouted, walking into the small room.

The intensity in his voice sent chills down Marty's spine.

Dee, Adam, and Lynn jerked upright and gasped. Jonathan turned quickly with an evil glint in his eyes.

"Let them go," Patch said.

Jonathan stood in silence for a moment. "Where's Trent? Ah, no matter, did the boy bring the map?"

"We brought it, but first, let them go," Patch said, standing in front of Marty.

Marty made eye contact with Dee. "Is everyone okay?"

Dee nodded.

"He's supposed to give me the map," Jonathan said, his voice deepening. "*Then*, they may leave."

"Jonathan," Patch said sternly, "or should I address you as Captain Morgan?"

Jonathan's attention rested solely on Patch. "What ever do you mean?"

"You know what I mean," Patch said. "Captain Morgan possesses you. It's not you, Jonathan, that would go to these extremes. You'd never hold children hostage or threaten them. You must resist his control. Find a way to thrust him out of you."

Jonathan blinked and shook his head slightly. For a moment, his confused gaze became less threatening, but it lasted only a few seconds. Jonathan's face tightened and his eyes glowed green. His voice deepened. "Since you know the truth, why goad me by refusing to give me the map. The treasure hidden is mine from long ago. It's rightfully mine."

Herman took courage and stepped between Patch and Jonathan, making himself fully visible, almost human in nature.

Jonathan snarled. "You! Cabin boy."

Jonathan rushed to grab Herman but his hands went through his ghostly figure.

Herman laughed. "You cannot touch or hurt me since you've taken control of a mortal."

Jonathan growled and turned toward Herman.

Herman continued his mocking laughter, further agitating and angering Captain Morgan. Herman pointed at Jonathan. "You tortured me even after I died, making me wander in isolation for centuries, but now, I have made friends. You're powerless now."

Again, Jonathan swooped his arms to grab the boy without any success.

Rage seethed in Jonathan, but it wasn't Jonathan's rage. The anger was so severe that the ghostly visage of Captain Morgan could be seen, prying itself free of his hold on Jonathan. Inside a physical form,

Morgan couldn't harm Herman. Marty wondered if Morgan could in his spirit form.

"You can't hurt me," Herman said, wailing with prideful laughter. "You no longer frighten me."

Jonathan staggered backwards and as he fell, Captain Morgan's spirit ripped free of Jonathan with a raging roar. Herman's laughter ceased. Fear consumed him, but before he could fade and become invisible, Morgan's huge ghostly hand wrapped around the boy's throat.

"I will pull you into the Underworld with me now, boy, and ensure you suffer for eternity!"

Dee stood. "Let him go!"

Morgan reared back his head, howling in fierce triumphant laughter. "None of you can stop me."

"I can," a voice said.

The room grew silent and all eyes turned to the ghostly appearance of Peg-leg Jack.

Captain Morgan released Herman. "It was you. You stole my treasure."

"Yes," Peg-leg replied. "And you killed me for it, which was the most foolish action to take. Dead men tell no tales. Surely, you'd heard of that long ago? So you hanged and killed me. You couldn't find it during your final years of life and you won't find it in your afterlife."

"Even in death, you're weaker than I," Captain Morgan said.

Jonathan sat up on the floor, holding his throat and gasping for air. George slipped to his friend and helped him move behind the table with Dee and the others.

A taunting grin spread on Peg-leg Jack's face. "Ah, perhaps not, Captain, but I didn't come alone."

Captain Morgan frowned in confusion.

Dee, Marty, and the rest of the living watched with widened eyes as dozens of ghosts entered the small room; their faces contorted by anger. Some ghosts were obviously other pirates, but some were from different centuries dressed in fancier clothes. All seethed staring at Morgan.

Captain Morgan studied their faces. "Few of these do I recognize."

Peg-leg Jack swept forward and stopped face-to-face with Morgan. "That's 'cause you robbed their graves searching for what I've hidden. Never violate the dead's resting places or the curses befall you."

"I set the curses," Morgan said. "They do not!"

Peg-leg Jack laughed. "You cursed yourself, damning others to their doom. But ya forgot one thing."

"What's that?"

"A restless spirit never crosses over. Not until vengeance is satisfied."

The dozens of ghosts encircled Captain Morgan and eased the circle tighter and tighter until Morgan's eyes widened with utmost dread.

Captain Morgan eyed various pirate ghosts and shouted, "This is mutiny!"

Peg-leg Jack grinned. "Long overdue."

The ghosts grabbed Morgan and pulled from different directions. He shouted and fought and squirmed, but he was unable to free himself. A dark spiraling circle opened near the wall. A vortex that led to eternal torment.

Morgan was turned to face the vortex and no longer made any threats. He pleaded to be released, but the vile pirate ghosts didn't hesitate. They pushed Morgan toward the vortex, but he seemed to have more strength than all of them combined and stopped their progress.

"You fools!" Morgan shouted, his eyes glowing red. "I'll destroy all of you!"

"Re-o-ow!" Pyewackett landed in the midst of the ghosts.

Seeing the black cat, Morgan shrieked with fear. His strength fled and he fell victim to the pirate ghosts. The ghosts plunged into the black circle, shoving Captain Morgan ahead of them. Morgan's screams silenced when the vortex shut.

Peg-leg Jack and a half dozen ghosts remained behind with Herman.

Dee slowly looked around the room. "Is it over?"

Peg-leg nodded. "Yes."

$\mathcal{M}$arty hurried to the table where Dee, Lynn, and Adam sat. The four embraced, forming a circle.

"I'm glad this is over," Marty whispered.

"Is that Patch?" Adam asked.

Marty nodded.

"Where's his eye-patch?" Dee asked.

"I'll tell you later," Marty said.

The lingering ghosts hovered at the edges of the room.

Peg-leg Jack returned.

Marty faced Jack. "Could you tell us what your buried treasure is?"

"Is it lots of gold?" Adam asked eagerly.

Patch grinned, seemingly also wondering.

"Ah, now," Peg-leg Jack said. "Part of the treasure was only valuable to Captain Morgan. I doubt it benefits any others."

"What did he value?" Dee asked.

"One was Captain Morgan's blessed compass, which he believed gave him luck on the high seas. I stole it on our journey to this cove, and well, it might be part of the reason for why the ship crashed. His obsession to find who stole it was the reason the ship struck the rocks. No one was at the wheel."

Patch grinned. "What's the other treasure?"

"A map to where he stashed shiploads of treasures on a remote isle in the angriest of seas. It was the only map he'd ever made of the location so he could return to the island. That's where the motherlode of gold rests."

"Another map?" Patch asked.

Jack nodded. "Aye."

Patch looked disheartened, as did Jonathan. "So the gold's never been in this cove?"

"No."

Patch shook his head and bellowed a deep laugh.

Marty and Dee stared at him in confusion.

Dee asked, "What's so funny?"

"I've wasted so many years looking for something that wasn't even here. Not that I didn't find some good stuff during that time, and I've had fun playing a treasure-hunting pirate."

Voices echoed down one of the tunnels and the flashing of lights washed across the walls, coming in their direction.

Pyewackett vanished, ensuring that only Marty was able to see the remaining ghosts.

Trent lowered his flashlight and two police officers stood behind him. A black welt encircled his left eye. Dried blood was crusted beneath his nose. "Here he is, officers."

Marty's stomach turned. He didn't want to see Patch arrested for assault and taking Trent's Jeep. But had Patch not done those things, Marty wasn't certain how the ordeal would've turned out. As much as Marty had tried to convince Trent to let him go, and even though Trent acted like he wanted to release Marty, Trent's fear of Jonathan prevented him from doing so.

Patch nervously glanced at the officers, but their attention wasn't on him. They walked to George and Jonathan and placed Jonathan in handcuffs.

"You kids all right?" one officer asked.

Dee and the others nodded.

The other officer patted George down and then placed him in

cuffs, too.

"What about Trent?" George asked.

"He's going to jail, too," the officer replied. "But from what he told us, you and he were threatened to cooperate in robbing these graves. If your stories collaborate, charges against you might be lessened for that offense."

"Feel free to ask me whatever you want," George said.

"Helping abduct teenagers, however, poses much bigger problems. I suggest you get good attorneys because no judge will view your actions favorable at all for that. You're still looking at time in prison," the officer said. "Come on, kids. We need to get you back to your parents."

CHAPTER 27

When the police walked Dee, Marty, Lynn, and Adam into the hotel lobby at 6:30 p.m., Terri and Glenda were perturbed. Dee was too afraid to meet her mother's gaze.

Dee recognized their mothers' angered stares for arriving at the hotel late, but some of her mother's anger stemmed from prolonged worry since she was unable to contact the teens.

"We're so sorry, mother," Dee said, rushing to embrace Terri.

Terri hugged Dee tightly. Her anger subsided and relief overshadowed her. Tears crested in her eyes. "You're all okay. That's what's important. You had us worried sick. We had already contacted the police."

The male and female officer smiled. "Dispatch notified us. That's why we rushed them here."

"Are they in any trouble?" Glenda asked, hugging Lynn.

"No," the officer replied. He explained what had happened with Jonathan and his two accomplices. "If anything, these kids deserve medals for their bravery. We'd have never discovered the tunnels under the graveyard without them finding the old treasure map. After one of the men drove Marty to the hotel to retrieve the map, Ol' Patch contacted us. He dresses like a scruffy one-eyed pirate on the beach while he uses his metal detector. He informs us whenever he sees suspicious people."

Terri looked at Marty and smiled. "You guys are full of surprises, aren't you?"

Marty shrugged.

Dee said, "Another mystery solved by Dee's Mystery Solvers!"

Terri grinned and shook her head. "I'm beginning to think this club of yours is going to get the four of you hurt … or worse."

"I agree," Glenda said.

"Perhaps we should discuss your disbanding the club after we get home," Terri said.

"What?" Dee said, pulling back from her mother's embrace. "No. We're having fun and—"

"We'll discuss it *later*, dear, when I'm not so tired and can think clearer," Terri said, patting the back of Dee's head. She stepped around Dee and shook hands with each officer and thanked them.

The female officer, Judi, said, "We'll need the kids to give us their statements. I can return in an hour, after you've eaten dinner, and get those, if that's okay with you."

Terri nodded. "Yes. That'll be fine."

CHAPTER 28

The next day, the trip home was long and glum. What should have been a triumphant achievement for Dee's Mystery Solvers was quashed by the possibility that their club would be dissolved by parental rule. Dee didn't like that and she sulked. She fought not to cry in front of everyone, but occasionally, a tear escaped.

Lynn held her conch shell and ran her fingers across the tiny grooves and indentions. From time to time, she glanced back at Marty but he slept with his head against the window.

Adam spent most of his time staring at his cellphone. His face seemed to reflect his self-examination of his lack of bravery during confrontation. He mumbled to himself while scrolling through topics on the phone's screen.

Dee opened her notebook and made notes for the next—and hopefully not their last—club meeting. After solving three mysteries, she was heartbroken to think they might not get to investigate any other odd occurrences.

She looked at the pictures of the Mystery Solvers standing on the sandy beach with Ol' Patch. Without the patch covering his eye, he wasn't as intimidating. With her mother's permission, they invited Patch to eat dinner with them in the hotel restaurant, and after his many stories of things he'd found buried in the sand, she found him an endearing person, much like her grandfather. Her mother and Lynn's enjoyed the dinner conversation.

Dee sniffled, writing down what she could remember of Patch's stories before the rich details faded. He promised if ever they returned to the Cove that he'd let them borrow one of his metal detectors so they could comb the beach to find treasure. She didn't know if they'd ever return, but she hoped they would.

She paused from writing and thought about Herman and the loneliness he'd endured for centuries. She couldn't imagine suffering that much pain and heartache. While some of the ghosts had vanished into the vortex with Captain Morgan, others walked through a lit open door that suddenly appeared. Some of the remaining ghosts passed through, no longer seeking retribution for Captain Morgan's atrocities. But, despite his isolation in the afterlife, Herman chose not to pass to the other side.

"Why are you staying?" Dee had asked him.

"Because I now have friends and family," Herman replied with a beaming smile.

"We're going back home," Marty said.

"I know." Herman pointed at the elderly ghost couple standing near the tunnel. "They said that they want to adopt me and give me the childhood I never got when I was alive. Of course, it won't be the same since I cannot experience physical interactions, but we can spend time together exploring places I've never been and see things I've never seen. I cannot do that if we pass through the doorway."

Dee smiled at his happiness. "But what if the door never shows for you again?"

Herman shrugged. "I don't know what awaits on the other side, but I know what's here. For all I know about what's beyond the doorway, I could slip into another place and be lonely again. I don't want to risk that possibility."

Herman looked at Marty and Pyewackett. "Thank you for all of your help."

Marty smiled.

The Mystery Solvers watched Herman glide to the elderly man and woman ghosts. He placed a hand into each of theirs and they disappeared through the tunnel.

Dee smiled. The Mystery Solvers might not have found any treasure, but seeing Herman finally happy with his new family was reward enough.

Dee drew circles on the corner of the paper.

"You guys are awfully quiet," Terri said, looking into the rearview mirror. "I know the trip wasn't what any of us expected, but I figured you'd all be chattering about your pictures being in the newspaper again."

"What's to be excited about," Dee said, softly. "You don't want our club to continue."

Terri sighed. "I was tired and worried and when we couldn't find you, I got agitated and a bit angry. I didn't mean to be so harsh and lash out about disbanding your club. The four of you are always going to be hanging around together. I've the feeling that if Glenda and I forbade you from having the club, you'd sneak around and do it anyways. But, we cannot stress the importance of not getting involved in dangerous situations."

"But this wasn't our fault," Dee said. "Marty found the bottle and map. All we were trying to do was find more information about the map and the possible treasure. That's almost any kid's fantasy, isn't it? We never expected to encounter someone like Jonathan. Honest. When he saw the bottle, he snapped and came after us."

"Right," Glenda said. "And *that's* when you should've contacted the police or other adults."

Terri nodded. "Or us."

"You were in a meeting," Dee said.

Marty aroused and rubbed his eyes.

"Dee," Terri said. "No meeting's more important than our kids if you're in a bad situation. If I see your number pop up on my phone, I won't hesitate to answer, regardless of what meeting I'm in. Because I know you won't call unless it's urgent. Let's get that clear."

"Yes, ma'am," Dee said.

"With that said," Terri looked into the mirror at Dee. "Your club may continue for a probationary period, but if future a investigation enters into a dangerous situation, all of you back away and inform us and the police. Understood?"

"Yes, ma'am," they all replied in near unison.

"Good. Now, get to discussing what all happened," Terri said. "It's been too quiet."

Dee smiled broadly. "Thanks, mother!"

All four of the Mystery Solvers straightened in their seats, recalling the order of events and teasing one another. Dee was glad they were as eager as she to keep the club active. She wondered what awaited them next. Only time could reveal such.

THE END

ABOUT THE AUTHOR

Leonard D. Hilley II grew up a quiet, shy kid with an inquisitive mind. Learning to read at an early age, he fell in love with books. He read every book he could get his hands on and stacks of dark comics about ghosts, monsters, and creepy things that stalk the night.

Like a lot of boys, he caught beetles, wooly bears, butterflies, and had an ant farm. When he was ten, his interests in science increased even more after seeing a professor's insect collection. Soon he set out on his quest to build his own collection. He also learned to rear butterflies and moths to obtain perfect specimens. He learned botany, gardening, and set his goal to become an entomologist.

At eleven, he saw Star Wars. His imagination soared. Soon after, he discovered Roger Zelazny's Chronicles of Amber. Six months later, he had written the first draft of a novel. A novel he later discarded, but the characters stuck with him. Years later, these characters came to life in Shawndirea, which Hilley intended to be a novella for Devils Den. The characters, however, refused to be ignored and took the opportunity to unveil Aetheaon in their first epic fantasy. Lady Squire: Dawn's Ascension was quick to follow.

Shawndirea was Hilley's farewell to butterfly collecting, and those who have read the novel understand why. He has taken Ray Bradbury's advice to heart: "Follow the characters." He does. He follows, listens, and take notes—often never knowing where they're going to take him, but he's never been disappointed in the results.

Hilley earned a B.S. in Biology and an MFA in Creative Writing to combine his love of science and writing.

Sci-fi Titles: Predators of Darkness: Aftermath, Beyond the Darkness, The Game of Pawns, Death's Valley, The Deimos Virus.

Epic Fantasy: Shawndirea (Aetheaon Chronicles: Book One), Lady Squire (Aetheaon Chronicles: Book Two), Frosthammer (Aetheaon Chronicles: Book Three), Shadowfae (Aetheaon Chronicles: Book Four), and Devils Den.

UF/PR: Succubus: Shadows of the Beast (Nocturnal Trinity Series: Book One), Raven (Nocturnal Trinity Series: Book Two)

YA UF/Paranormal: Forrest Wollinsky Vampire Hunter; Forrest Wollinsky: Blood Mists of London; Forrest Wollinsky: Predestined Crossroads.